SPRUCE ROAD

Scott R.S. Raphael

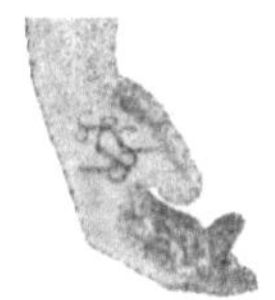

Dedicated to:

Boo, Bae, & Bitch

Contents

SPRUCE ROAD

1. Nowhere

"YOU KNOW WHAT the only thing I hate more than bad drivers is?" Mick began in a drole monotone, glancing at Brady, lazed back in the passenger seat, halfway through his second spliff of the drive. "BAD DRIVERS WHO ARE IN MY WAY!" He smacked the horn so quickly it barely blipped.

"Bu-uu-uu-dy." Brady laughed. "Calm down." He sucked in deeply and blew the smoke half out the semi-cracked window and half into the face of Gavin, seated behind him and trying not to choke on the fumes.

"I'll calm down," Mick returned to his typical monotone, "when they get out of my…"—he jerked the wheel to the right to avoid a braking SUV— "…way."

Gavin grabbed the door for support and still managed to smack his head against the window. Brady hardly seemed to notice the movement.

Probably a good thing you don't have to drive behind your-self, Gavin thought, but he wouldn't say it aloud. He didn't know Brady or Mick well enough to make the jab and, frankly, he wasn't that comfortable with how long they'd been stuck in traffic together. Travis was supposed to have driven him up to the cottage weekend with Alyssa and Mav, but he'd just had to plough his car through a maple tree after a wild night at *Bar Muerte*, leading to a complete reorganization of seating arrangements, and thirteen stitches in the noggin.

"You remember when you used to like driving just for the fun of it?" Brady poked Mick playfully in the shoulder.

"Oh, you mean when I was sixteen and didn't have anywhere to be?"

"And how old are you now? Seventeen? We ain't in no rush."

"Look, just because you're an old man…"

"Guy, I will be an old man when I am thirty, *if* I feel like making it that long," Brady tilted his seat back further, crushing Gavin's knees, but he didn't dare protest.

"What are you, five years older than me?"

Brady just shrugged. "Who knows? Numbers."

"Numbers," Mick concurred as Gavin did some quick mental math, pegging Brady at twenty-eight and Mick at twenty-three, putting him in the middle at twenty-five and a half. And that half mattered. For some reason.

"You missed the turn off," Brady offered uselessly, checking the map on his phone for the first time in fifteen minutes.

"Seriously? Who made you navigator?"

"Not me. Blame backseat." He jabbed a thumb in Gavin's direction.

Gavin raised his arms in mock offense, "I have a name, you know?"

"I'm starting to think we should've let *Gavin navi*gate." Mick chuckled silently at his joke before turning back to dead serious. "Now, where the hell do I go? We were making record time."

"Look, all I know is, the map said it'd take two hours, and that passed thirty minutes ago."

"Just get me back on track…"

"You just missed a right."

"You didn't tell…ugh, whatever, you know. At least we're having a good time; relaxing Friday afternoon drive up to the country and—SIGNAL, ASSHOLE!"

"Next right, then merge into express." Brady scanned over the turn list. "We're almost there, anyway. Just need to get out of known civilization by about twenty miles, first."

"Why did Kaylyn need to have her birthday weekend in the middle of nowhere, anyway?" Mick glanced at the gas gauge, decided it was full enough to be Sunday's problem.

"Oh, true. Forgot it was Kaylyn's birthday."

"Dude, she invited you. How did you forget that?"

"I dunno, probably high or something."

"What did you think we were going for?"

"Beach, swimming, barbeque burgers, whatever."

Mick glanced over at Brady again, wishing he didn't have to wear sunglasses to combat the setting sun so that his friend and co-worker could see the what's-wrong-with-you look on his face. "It's November."

"Look, it's sixty degrees out, and all I know is, if its fifty-five, you go outside."

"Sixty-five. Maybe."

"Fifty-five. Don't be soft, white boy."

"Soft? Fifty-five is basically a freezer. Gavin, settle it."

Gavin snapped out of his daydream and took a moment to clue in. "Uh, I don't know."

"Cop out, pick one," Mick insisted, and even with the sunglasses on, Gavin could've sworn he saw a threat in the driver's eyes in the rear-view mirror.

"I guess sixty-five…"

"Wait, wait, wait," Brady cut in. "Doesn't count. Gavin works in the kitchen, he's used to the heat." Indeed, Gavin worked in the kitchen at Asher's Palace, where Mick tended bar and Brady served as a sommelier-in-training, rendering them the tightest-knit pair in the restaurant. Truthfully, though, he felt better getting away from the ovens than into them.

"Turn left," Brady instructed, and Mick did.

Then, the world fell away.

From cars and traffic and civilization and people, it was as though they'd broken through a barrier in time and space and come out in the reverse of the universe they'd long known. The road turned dirt and Mick cursed as they bounced violently over a tree root. "I swear, if my muffler's busted, Kaylyn's not getting a birthday present this year."

The trees converged to shroud their journey and when they burst free into barren emptiness a few miles later, the sky had started to turn. "I don't wanna still be driving when it's dark."

"It's cool. Maybe fifteen more miles."

"I'm gunning it." Mick accelerated, blowing through a tiny town of five or seven buildings. His eyes focussed on the road, he could've sworn the woman outside the bank was watching them. Still watching them, a mile past. He tried to shake it off. "How much alcohol'd you guys bring? Should I go back and stop for anything?" He didn't want to go back, but he also felt like he was supposed to, for some reason. That forward was a mistake.

"I'm fully stocked." Brady patted a bag at his feet.

"I'm good," Gavin confirmed. "What happened to getting there ASAP?"

"Yeah, no, just checking. We're still gonna make great time."

They shot back into the forest, Mick turning his hands around the wheel as he curled winding roads at speeds only a local should have been taking.

It would be good to get away, he thought. The restaurant had taken a lot out of him and his tips had to go to something other than schooling. He was never going to do better than bartending, after all. Why keep wasting it all without any fun?

Twilight bit across the sky and a few maple leaves that had stubbornly clung to their branches through the bulk of autumn finally made their dance to the ground around them.

"I've been trying to figure out," Mick said, after an extended silence, "what was"—not *unsettling* or *uncomfortable*; he couldn't use those words even though they felt right—"*different* about this place." He hesitated to listen one more time, to confirm. "It's quiet. It's *way* too quiet."

"Welcome to the country, my guy."

"Man, I grew up on a farm in the south for the first ten years of my life. I know quiet. This isn't that.

Out there, there's no sound. Here: it's like something's eating the sound, if that makes sense…" He looked to Brady for some kind of confirmation and got a shrug. To Gavin. But all he received was a look of shock, a point, and a cry of "WATCH OUT!"

Mick snapped his neck around just in time to see a tall, lumbering figure, limping slowly down the middle of the road, clad all in black. Half-an-hour later and he would've been invisible if not for the headlights. Mick whipped the wheel to the left, sending the back wheels into a tailspin.

Pumping the brakes and tearing at the steering wheel, he somehow managed to right the car just as it was about to fly into a ditch at the side of the road. Heart beating fast, he accelerated as quickly as he could past the figure, who took no notice of the fact that he'd nearly been crushed at eighty miles an hour. Just continued trudging along.

Risking a glance back, Mick tried to make out the man's face, but in the now-near-blackness, he could see little more than a hood and shadow. "What…" he began, voice cracking slightly before he coughed and righted himself. "What're you doing in the middle of the road, buddy?"

The others said nothing.

Mick whipped around another corner, deeper into the forest, just wanting the drive to be over.

"Take a right on Spruce Road…I think. My data's cutting in and out."

"There is no right."

"I don't know, take the next right."

"Hold it up or something. Gavin, you have a connection?"

"Nothing," Gavin glanced quickly at the phone he'd been avoiding for the past two hours, anxious as to what his notifications might have brought.

"Great, so we'll just…" And as if a veil had lifted and the world around them had morphed once more, a right turn appeared from between the bushes. Mick made a sharp turn and skidded slightly, knocking the phone from Gavin's hand and leaving him fishing beneath his seat.

In the distance, there was a light. Then two, then three.

And as the car ground to a halt along the gravel driveway that separated a few dozen feet of land from the mass of natural paths around it, the three young men looked up upon a house much vaster and more majestic than they could have imagined.

It was hard to make out much in the dark, but a single streetlight sat outside, to guide the wayward traveller, casting just enough light to let them know that the top and edges of the house were spread so far apart that they disappeared into the darkness.

As Mick turned at a right angle to park next to the car that was already in the drive, the headlights peeled across a rundown post bearing the misnomer "The Little Maple Cabin". Then, like much else, the world was cast into darkness, as Mick shut off the ignition and opened the door upon the new and mysterious realm before them.

2. Preparation

KAYLYN SINGH FELT like she was going to pass out, but she wasn't going to stop. Not now, not when this was taking forever, as it was. With a deep breath, she closed her eyes, paused, and exhaled with all her might.

The balloon exploded in her hand with an enormous pop that brought the eyes of her boyfriend, Dorian, and her best friend, Mallory, shooting up in shock. "Well, thanks for that!" Mallory rubbed an ear gingerly.

"Are you kidding me? Are you *kidding* me?" Kaylyn exclaimed, jumping up from her seat and aggressively grabbing at the pieces of balloon, depositing them into a nearby trashcan, with violence.

"It's okay, babe." Dorian slid over and placed a hand on the heart of her back, guiding her back to the couches in the middle of the massive living room. "Just sit down and take a breather."

She shuddered his hand off and sat down. Dorian took the hint and kept his distance while Mallory surreptitiously returned to blowing up a balloon of her own. After a moment of silence, Kaylyn settled slightly, though she was still tense. "I just want it to be perfect. I *need* everything to be perfect."

"Look around you," Dorian soothed, gesturing to the room at large. "Everything's already going perfect."

Kaylyn took another searching glance around the room, taking in the sixty-inch, 4K flat screen; the six-panel floor-to-ceiling windows that looked out onto the patio, surrounded by tall, vibrant hedges; the marble kitchen island, long enough to prepare three meals on simultaneously; the open footage that could easily host double, even triple the thirteen impending guests in this single room, with space to spare. "I'm really happy with the cottage. I'm really happy with the space," she repeated. "This is…even better than I expected from the pictures online."

"See, everything's gonna go fine. It's like that picture says"—Dorian gestured to a photo of a beach, a motivational message scrawled across the sand—"'The sand only burns until the flame inside glows hotter.'"

Kaylyn looked at the photo, blinked.

"Take it down?" Dorian inferred.

"Take it down."

Mallory finished inflating another balloon and tossed it into the pile in front of her. "Don't worry, we're going to get everything done in no time. It'd be nice if we had a little *help*, though." Her eyes darted to the staircase down to the basement.

"Whatever, I'm over it." Kaylyn picked up another balloon and started blowing.

"No, they should be up here helping, like the rest of us."

"I mean, yeah"—Kaylyn puffed—"but we knew…"—puff—"…what we were getting…"—puff—"…when we invited…"—puff—"…Irina." Kaylyn tied the balloon off with a wash of relief.

"Why *did* you invite her?" Mallory adjusted her glasses and raised an eyebrow at her best friend.

Kaylyn dropped her voice to a whisper, though she was sure they'd never be able to hear her all the way downstairs in this cavernous place. "I mean, we all like Malachi, and it's kinda hard to invite him and not his girlfriend, especially when we've known her longer."

"So? I mean, we were never *friends* with her, before she started dating Malachi. Now, she just tags along."

"Whatever." Kaylyn had no interest in wasting any more of her precious time dwelling on it. "It's another body to split the cost of the weekend. We'll probably barely see her, anyway."

Mallory collapsed back, starting to unfurl a large "HAPPY BIRTHDAY" poster that was three times the size of her five-foot-nothing frame. "I just wish she wasn't a manager, then we wouldn't have to be nice to her."

"Not like I care, anymore," Kaylyn mused, getting up in search of the best place to hang the poster, now wrapped around Mallory's right leg and left arm as she tried to disentangle herself without tearing the thing to shreds.

"Oh yeah, just keep rubbing it in that you got a big girl job and finally got to quit."

Kaylyn grinned to herself as she scoured the room. Kaylyn Singh, Wedding Planner. It had a nice ring to it. Okay, Kaylyn Singh, *Associate* Wedding Planner. But one thing led to another. And when her break finally came, she knew that no one would forget her name.

"Oh, you'll get there one day; we all do." Dorian joined Kaylyn in the search, shooting a slightly-irritating-but-probably-well-intentioned smile back at Mallory, now even more entangled than before.

"Okay, but at least you never worked at the Palace that long, Dorian. You were only there—what?—a year?"

"Eight months."

"Eight months. That's barely enough time to have Chef Jorge bust your balls *and* wear them as a necklace. I've been stuck there for seven *years* and am going to die there." The groan in her voice betrayed a much deeper sentiment that no one could miss, but the sardonic tone that she had mastered over the years made it easy to ignore.

"Gotta keep moving. It's not good for me to stay in one place for too long. But anyway, don't worry," Dorian brushed it off, "you don't even have balls to bust. You'll be fine."

"Thanks, Dorian." And she almost sounded like she meant it, although she most certainly did not.

A car door slammed in the distance and the sound was immediately consumed by the night. "Just in time to blow up the last of the balloons!" Kaylyn declared as Mick led a nervous-looking Gavin and a much-too-relaxed Brady into the living room.

"Well, hello to you, too." Mick laughed, removing his sunglasses, which he only now realized he'd never taken off, even through the blackest stretches of the drive. Blinded, yet still able to see.

He shook his head quickly and refocussed on the room, just in time to see a balloon hit him in the nose. Recovering, he batted it back toward Gavin, who was now in the process of attempting to blow up two balloons at once, while still participating in the makeshift game.

"Where the drinks go?" Brady focussed on the important matters.

"Um, the fridge." Kaylyn gestured obviously to the corner of the room.

"Or your stomach," Mick corrected.

"Did I hear the Boozy Boys come in?" Malachi Joseph jogged up the stairs to say hi to the group. In the time since his arrival, the three-hundred-pound teddy bear had changed from jeans into track pants, and he greeted the room with an air hug any three-year-old would've loved to take to bed with them.

"Mister Manager." Brady clapped his hand, and when met with a slightly confused look, clarified. "You shack up with Miss Manager, you become Mister Manager."

"And here I was, thinking I'd gotten a promotion."

"Keep dreaming, busboy." Brady gave him a jab on the arm and offered him a drag on his latest joint.

"Can you do that outside?" Kaylyn waved smoke from her face, though she was nowhere near to the flame.

Brady headed for the back porch. "Not that way," Dorian advised, gesturing to a sign that read *HAZARD: DO NOT USE PORCH!* Brady acknowledged him with a grateful finger gun and headed straight back out the front door.

"Irina coming up?" Mick asked. Mallory covered her mouth to suppress the scoff.

"No, no…" Malachi glanced back downstairs. "She's tired. But she'll be up in a bit. Long night."

"Probably a good time for us to get away, then," Dorian said, a twinkle in his deep blue eyes. "I know I've needed to get away for a *long* time."

"Yeah, you know," Malachi carried on justifying, "some family troubles, issues with her brother. Guy's kind of a dick. You know how it goes."

"Yeah." Kaylyn smiled kindly, a master of the art of decorum, when she cared to practice. "No rush for her to come up; the party hasn't started yet." She tossed him a balloon. "But now you're here, you can help us get ready."

Malachi glanced down the stairs again. "Yeah, of course," he started to blow, nervously.

Gavin felt a hand upon his shoulder and, a moment later, Mallory had dragged him behind the kitchen island. "Hey, what's up?" He tried to return his close friend's clearly put-on smile.

"Oh, nothing much…good ride up?"

Gavin shot a quick look at Mick and found him engaged in a one-man round of Keep the Balloon Up, well away from the rest of the party. Still, he dropped his voice to a whisper. "Yeah, I mean…I think I might have a concussion, but other than that."

"That good, huh?"

"Yeah, well…" He looked around once more. "I didn't want to say anything because I know Kaylyn was super stressed out with all the planning and driver changes and stuff, but…I'd kinda been hoping to come up with her, you, Travis, or Mav. Would've been a bit more comfortable, for conversation and everything."

"Well, you definitely wouldn't've had to worry about conversation if you'd been with us." Mallory grinned with malice. "Not *your* conversation, necessarily, but *someone* would've been talking the whole way up."

"That bad?"

"I swear." Mallory slammed a hand down on the kitchen island more loudly than intended and looked around to make sure that no one had noticed. She lowered her voice further. "I swear, Irina wouldn't shut up the whole way here. First, she was backseat driving, then she was complaining about the route, the temperature. Then—*then*—she took a forty-five-minute phone call for an argument, in Russian, on speaker phone."

"If it was in Russian, how'd you know she was arguing?" Gavin smirked.

"Oh." Mallory waved her hands dramatically. "No. *She* wasn't arguing. She was *mediating* between two other people on the call who were having an argument with each other. And guess who had to jack the volume up to freakin' eleven." She paused to think. "And she kept kicking the back of Dorian's seat, while he was driving. I think that might've been an accident, but it happened *way* too often."

"So, I guess I'll take my concussion."

"I *wish* I'd been knocked out for that trip." She took a deep breath, relieved to finally have that out of her system.

"All right, all right." Gavin nodded, giving her time to cool off. "It's all good now. We can finally relax."

From the door, a loud crash cut through the entire building, booming into the silence around them with pervasive insistence. Again. And again. *BOOM! BOOM! BOOM!*

The room went quiet. Glances were exchanged. Malachi hiccoughed, grabbed his heart, needed to sit down. Instinctively, Mick put everyone behind him, looking to the door defensively.

Unphased, Kaylyn walked past them all and casually moved to the door, as though nothing alarming or unexpected had occurred. Everyone gathered around. Everyone but Malachi, still trying to recover his weak heart. Softly, Kaylyn turned the handle as the wind took the door in and nearly blew her arm off with it.

Before them, silhouetted in the light of the single streetlamp, stood a giant of a man. Seven-foot-tall, hooded, unidentifiable.

But Mick didn't need to look twice to know precisely who stood before them: the figure from the street, the one he'd nearly run down along the dark forested path. The faceless man with no concept of—or maybe, worse, no concern for—the death that came inches from taking him.

Without waiting for an invitation, he took a step across the threshold. And no one would dare ask him to stop. He raised two hands wide enough to crush a neck in a single squeeze and slowly lowered his hood to reveal a hard and haunted face, blanched white and sunken. He may once have been handsome. He may still have been, if not for whatever had possessed his soul.

Slowly, almost creakingly, his lips curled into a taut smile. "Hello," he began in a slow, deep, booming voice. "I'm DJ. Welcome to my cottage."

3. Tour

"YOU MUST BE…Kaylyn Singh." DJ's gaze fixed upon Kaylyn. "Happy birthday." There was no pleasure in his tone. "Thank you for booking with me. I hope you'll enjoy your stay." Every word he spoke seemed to drag into oblivion, slowing as his sentence stretched on.

With a swallow, Kaylyn managed, "You have a very nice home."

DJ's lips pursed, as though the thought perturbed him. "This…is not my home." And Gavin could've sworn he heard him mutter beneath his breath, "It should make no home for the living," before he carried on with, "My home is just down the street, two miles to the south. If you should ever need anything during your stay, please don't hesitate to knock. You can't miss it. No one else lives here."

"Thanks, I'm sure everything will be great, though." Dorian clapped a hand around Kaylyn's shoulder and smiled warmly, but a hint of *can you leave us alone, please?* hung in his tone.

DJ smiled without warmth or happiness. "Indeed. Now, if I may, I feel it's usually best to give my guests a tour of the grounds. Only too much can go wrong when improperly prepared." British—that was what Gavin had been trying to figure out all along. There was a British lilt to DJ's voice, but it was very faint, as of one who hadn't visited the homeland, or people at all, in fifty years, though the man who stood before them couldn't have been more than thirty-seven or eight.

"That'd be great," Dorian chimed in again, trying to end the exchange quickly and return to party preparation.

DJ pressed through the group to the centre of the room. No one was quite sure whether they were meant to follow. Finally, with a glance at the rest of the crowd and a shrug, Mick took up after DJ and the others fell in line. They stopped at the kitchen. "These burners"—DJ waved a hand overtop the 1950s-style oven casually—"get very hot. If they set off the alarms, wave them down quickly or the fire department will come. If the fire department comes, you will be asked to leave."

Without a look at those around him, DJ swept across the hall to the wall of windows, gently turning a switch that none of them had seen and illuminating a flickering incandescent bulb beyond the panes. "This porch is unfit for use. The wood is rotten. You *will* fall through. You have been warned. If an ambulance is called, you will be asked to leave."

"Is that a camera?" Malachi gestured to a small, blinking contraption in the upper corner of the deck.

DJ whipped around to face Malachi with a hard, cold look, shutting out the light behind him—or maybe the dying bulb had merely drawn its final breath. "It's a heat sensor and nothing more," he snarled. "You will not be watched and I am no pervert."

Malachi took a step backward. "Okie-dokie, then…"

"Why do you need a heat sensor?" Mick inquired, clearly unintimidated by the giant before them.

DJ blinked once. "To watch for…discrepancies…"

"Discrepancies in what?"

"The air." But DJ had no further time for this line of questioning and was already trudging down the staircase by the front door. Malachi winced, wanting to warn Irina but not entirely sure how. Accepting his best option was simply to be there to soften the blow, he pressed through his hesitation and rushed to follow closely.

And he nearly rammed into DJ's back after an abrupt stop at the base of the stairs. "The basement gets cold at night. Very cold. And, sometimes, during the day. If you're in this room"—he walked through a set of double doors to the left and into a bare bedroom with three beds against the far wall, positioned directly below three high windows—"you may find the sounds of the house are loudest."

Kaylyn whispered in Gavin's ear, "This is you, Mallory, and Mav's room," and Gavin bit his lower lip to discourage protest as a draft swept through the doors.

"You may hear the boiler or the sump pump— they waken some, at all hours. Or, you might hear something else." His all-black ensemble billowed behind him as he drifted seamlessly out of the room and into a hidden space on the right, also containing one large bed, directly under a window. "In here, you may see shadows. Usually, it's the trees outside."

That was all he had to say about the room. Kaylyn whispered methodically under her breath, "Travis and Alyssa's room."

In the main basement, DJ led them past two over-stuffed couches, an old, run-down video game console that appeared to be missing its joystick, a poster of an iguana advertising, 'Iguanas have cold blood, yet hate the cold. Don't let your makeup define you', and a television that reflected their shirts and distorted their faces as they passed.

"What's through those doors?" Mick gestured toward two rooms they had passed on their right.

"The boiler room," DJ responded without looking around.

"Both of them?"

"The one on the left."

"What about the other door?" Mick pressed.

DJ turned so quickly on his heel that none of the group realized that he was facing them until they caught a glimpse of his sunken, grey eyes staring through them. He stood still for a moment, as if buffering, and then his eyes drifted slowly, harshly toward the right-side door, separated from its partner by a side table and a disconcerting photo of a cat suckling a pacifier and wearing a bonnet, reading, "The cradle won't rock itself."

"Nothing," DJ finally pronounced, reinserting the air that had been sucked out of the room. "Nothing's in there."

With that, he returned to his tour, not noticing as Mick casually tried the handle on the way past and found it locked.

Before them sat a small bathroom, apparently the one compressed room in the house, completely dark but for a small LED flashlight plugged into a wall outlet, slowly changing from red light to green to purple to red again. Apparently with nothing to say about this area, DJ introduced the door to the right ("Brady and Mick's room," per Kaylyn).

"Here, you'll hear nothing. These walls have never liked sound. They never will."

As the rest of the group left the room, Mick paused to peruse his quarters, noting that—in contrast to the others they'd seen so far, these two beds were not next to each other, nor directly under windows. One's head sat against one wall, in the corner. And the other's against the opposite wall, in the opposite corner. A line could have been drawn on a diagonal down the centre of the room, with each side being symmetrical. "Glad it's just two nights," Mick hummed, but no one was around to hear, and no one could have in that room, if what DJ said was true.

Across the hall, Malachi cried out, "Wait!" as DJ reached for the door to his and Irina's room, but DJ had no interest in his pleas. He threw the door aside to reveal a stunned and half-naked Irina, clad in just black underwear, in the midst of applying lotion to her long, slender legs. She shrieked and uttered a Russian oath before instinctively covering her chest with both hands. DJ seemed to take no notice. "This is the only bedroom with a lock on it," he proclaimed.

Irina cursed him, "And you could not have told me this before?" She spat on the floor, eyes staring falcon-like through Malachi as he rushed to get her a shirt, whispering unaccepted apologies under his breath. "And, just who the hell are you?"

"I am the owner," DJ replied calmly, barely noticing her as she quickly pulled on one of Malachi's twelve-times-too-large shirts.

"Well, that is a one-star review for you!" she declared, the shirt billowing behind her size-zero frame as she stepped forward aggressively.

Kaylyn laughed nervously. "No, no, so funny, ha!"

"And the rest of you"—Irina's black eyes opened to their fullest, gaping size, pupils contracting—"GET THE HELL OUT OF MY BEDROOM!"

DJ took a moment of pause—he would not be told—before finally turning and walking slowly from the room. With another apologetic look, Malachi shut the door behind them.

The basement completed, they returned to the main level, where DJ gestured to his right with a casual, "There's a bathroom and two bedrooms there."

"Mine and Dorian's; Torri and Jim's," Kaylyn finished her list.

"You'll find nothing of consequence there." DJ started for the front door before adding one final comment about the interior. "But, if you *do* happen to find something of note, do let me know."

Gavin cleared his throat nervously to ask the question on all of their minds, but couldn't find his voice for fear of the answer. Mick picked up the slack: "What would we find?"

"That's just it," DJ mused, "one never knows. But every now and again, the guests will notice something...out of place. I really must know, that I may...work with it."

From there he ventured into the chilled November night, nearly knocking over Brady, just having finished his smoke break. "Who's that guy?" He jerked his thumb in DJ's direction as the rest of the group followed dazedly behind.

"Owner, apparently," Mick said, some doubt creeping into his otherwise casual tone.

"Oh, cool. Why's he creepy as hell?"

Kaylyn shushed him aggressively. "He might be able to hear you."

"I don't care." Brady shrugged, before calling loudly to the front of the pack, "Hey buddy, why you so creepy?"

With a small, creeping smile that sickeningly infiltrated his every word, DJ called back over his shoulder, "I wish, wholly, that you shall never understand."

"Cool, cool." Brady patted Mick on the shoulder. "I'm out." He pointed a finger gun at Gavin. "Keep me updated on whacko." And he breezed back into the house, slamming the door behind him.

"If there are more to your party," DJ hummed as he led them around the side of the large grounds, along a row of trees, and into an overgrown opening that doubled as the backyard, "do ensure that they know of these important details. I would hate for there to be any...unexpected incidents."

And just as silently as they all agreed not to speak of this tour again, they equally understood that no one ought to ask, "Like what?"

The weeds grew long and, in the dark of a nearly moonless night, they could have entered the void and never have known the difference. Ahead, DJ lit a flashlight and they followed that light of salvation into oblivion.

The light descended.

At the front of the pack, Dorian and Mallory felt nervously about for a ledge before finding a previously invisible, jagged, stone staircase. Dorian took Kaylyn's hand and Mallory grabbed at passers before they could tumble to their deaths.

Slowly, feeling out the stairs that DJ took with ease, they made their way to the base of the steps, which, though few in number, seemed to take hours to brave.

Gavin screamed, a high-pitched cry in the night. Something cawed in the distance. Mallory reached out blindly and just managed to catch his arm as he careened past, dragging them both downward.

Hands thrust desperately forward, Gavin sought an unseeable ground. And found it almost instantly. Mallory crashed down hard upon his bony back.

"All good?" Mick dragged the pair back up, one by one.

"Yeah," Gavin replied sheepishly. "Missed a step."

"Good thing it was the last one," Dorian chimed in from the front. He may have turned around at the sound, he may not have. No one could have known in this dark.

They followed the light until DJ cried, "Stop!" and no one dared take another step. "Beyond this ledge"—he drew the flashlight along a rocky corner, just inches from his toes—"is the lake. The fall is seventy-two feet. Five have gone over, in my time at this place. Four have died."

"And the other?" Mick toed at the edge until a rock fell away.

"No one knows." DJ turned back swiftly, and everyone took care as they did the same. "The final stop on our tour"—he pointed the flashlight at a stony circle a few feet away—"is the firepit. Do remember to put out your fires when you've finished. The trees may have the quietest voices in these parts, but you'll never escape their screams if the forest should go up in flames. The sand pits are over there." He flicked the flashlight to a distant pile. "And if you should need water, I would recommend acquiring it from the faucet, and not from down there." He moved the flashlight back to the cliff's edge.

They waited in collective silence, prepared for the warning to follow. But instead, DJ said, "That was a joke."

No laughter followed.

Wordlessly, DJ led the group back to the front of the house, where the single streetlight glared as brightly as the sun to their darkened eyes. "This is where I leave you, and I do hope you enjoy your stay. There's only one more thing that I must ask before I go." Half of the group had already ventured up the steps toward the front door, and the rest were envious of their distance from the host. But, still, all turned for this final tidbit of DJ's intrusion:

"Would you like to hear about the ghost?"

This time, laughter accompanied the comment. Some of it nervous, all of it uncomfortable. Mick smiled as he led Dorian, Malachi, and Kaylyn back inside, calling back, "Good one, but no."

"Ghost?" Gavin swallowed hard.

"Come on." Mallory placed a hand in the centre of his back and guided him toward the front door, glancing back at DJ's imposing figure, silhouetted against the single streetlight, before looking away quickly.

DJ looked on as they retreated, contemplating quietly. "How brave you all must be," he mused, and Gavin tried to turn back, but Mallory kept guiding. "In my long time here, no soul has stayed in this house beyond a single night. I wish you all the best."

Gavin finally broke away and charged for the retreating host. "Tell me! What's going on?"

But DJ had already disappeared into the black of the night, and not another sound lived on Spruce Road.

4. Recovery

"I DON'T KNOW. I don't like it." Gavin smacked the balloon as hard as he could, which wasn't particularly hard, and it tailed off low so that Mick had to dive to keep it from hitting the ground.

"Come on, the guy was having a joke with us the whole time." Gavin recovered poorly, again, and Mick was sent on another run.

"It didn't feel like it."

"The guy literally said he was joking," Mick pointed out.

"About jumping off a cliff," Gavin clarified, pounding his stress out on the balloon. "Literally, the only joke he made was about jumping off a cliff."

"I wouldn't worry about it, man. If he's not joking, he's a nut. It's one or the other."

"And then? He comes and kills us in our sleep? That's not better."

"Pretty sure there'd be some more one-star reviews of this place if the host was a murderer." Mick laughed softly to himself.

"From who, their ghosts?"

Mick hesitated and almost missed the balloon. "Fair point."

"I need a drink," Gavin moaned. "When's Travis getting here?"

With a shrug and a yawn, Mick made a lighter return than usual. "Couple more hits and I'm going to bed."

"Um…" Gavin glanced the balloon off his finger and leapt for it just as it was about to hit the ground. "…It's, like, seven-thirty."

"Yeah, I got…"—*yawn*—"…sleeping problems. And I've been up since five-thirty for my other job."

"What do you do again?"

"It's a freelance cleaning service. Like, apartments and BnBs and stuff. You wouldn't believe the amount of blood, piss, and semen I deal with every day."

After another balloon strike, Gavin subconsciously wiped his hand on his shirt. "And then you go and serve people handmade drinks."

"It's not like I'm stirring with my finger. Besides, I wash my hands. Most of the time." Mick smacked the balloon as high as he could into the air. "Last to touch before it hits the ground wins."

*

"I THINK WE should take down the weird lion photo and put up some streamers, for photos." Kaylyn looked around the room as she continued blowing up the last of the balloons from her spot on one of the three couches in the middle of the room.

On the middle couch, Mallory brushed a strand of red hair from under her glasses as she tried to open a package of party horns. "I think Dorian tried earlier and it wouldn't come down."

"Of course, it wouldn't, of all things."

"That DJ guy probably doesn't want anyone stealing it."

"I'd rather have a blank wall."

On the third couch, Brady lazed back and unconsciously lit up another spliff. He took a long drag before noticing the silence around him and eyeing Kaylyn and Mallory's unamused faces.

"Oh, right. You want some, birthday girl?" He held the joint over the table.

"Um, no…" replied a slightly stupefied Kaylyn, whose distaste for the practice and long-held oath never to smoke a substance of any kind—though she might drink what she was able—was common knowledge amongst those of even her most fleeting acquaintance.

Taking it in stride, and taking another suck, Brady pointed to her. "Oh, yeah. By the way. Sorry 'bout your parents."

Kaylyn stopped halfway through blowing up a balloon, her face going stony as the air slowly trickled out between her thumb and forefinger. "Yeah, um, thanks…" She tried to blow again, but with less heart than before.

Mallory shot Brady a look, but he didn't see. "I mean, that's crazy. Like, do you know what…?" Now he saw Mallory's searing gaze, though he had little choice once she'd kicked him in the shin.

"Right, yeah, sorry, you want some?" he offered her the spliff.

Mallory turned away in disgust and returned to breaking a fingernail on the stubborn package of party horns. Neither woman had the energy to tell Brady to smoke outside.

*

THE BASEMENT WAS cold, colder than Dorian
had expected, even with the warnings given. Not
wanting to disturb anyone with his exploration, he'd
left the lights out, hoping to be able to see his way in
the faint glimmer coming from upstairs. It only half-
worked and he could make out little more than silhouettes of his surroundings.

He dragged his fingertips loosely against the wall,
keeping a safe distance from it, lest he bump into an
invisible table. As he moved further and further into
the darkness, the world seemed to become colder, until he was nearly shivering.

Still, he kept his fingers in place, even as his hand
wanted to close in upon itself for warmth, letting the
friction burn against his fingertips and trying to chan-
nel that energy into the rest of his body.

He came upon the boiler room door and, turning
the handle very slowly, slipped inside and shut the
door behind himself. Small red lights provided the
sole illumination in the otherwise black room, and the
tiny lightbulb that flickered on when he flipped the
switch did little more than expose the shadows. His
socks picked up rocks and detritus from the scratchy,
concrete floor as he ventured past the boiler into the
dark corners of the room, where he was forced to feel
about blindly, once more. A broom, a vacuum, a
plunger caked in dust. Nothing of much interest.

The boiler screeched with a kettling noise that
made the young man jump and grab his heart as he
shook his head at his own stupidity.

With nothing of interest to find, he edged back along the wall and out the door once more, closing it as quietly as he could.

Dorian curled his way around a short table and continued along the wall until he came upon the neighbouring door.

He turned the handle slowly but found it locked. Or maybe stuck? He yanked harder, harder. But it wouldn't budge. Scraping a thumb along the centre of the handle, he found no lock. Nor was there one above or below.

Locked from the inside? With no other way into the room? It just could not have been!

He tried again to pry the door open. There had to be something within. He refused to believe DJ's brush off of "nothing."

Dorian put his foot against the doorframe and pushed hard as he pulled. It wouldn't move.

He felt a touch upon his shoulder. Soft at first, but then firm, clutching. He whipped around, pressing his back hard against the door.

Irina stood before him, tall and ghostly white, even in the black of the basement. She dragged a long false fingernail from his shoulder down to the centre of his chest and tapped him, twice. "What are you doing down here?" Her thick, deep Russian accent rendered the most innocent of questions demanding. But then, the hard look in her eyes suggested that it was most certainly more than just a question.

"Just looking around, wanted to see what was down here."

Irina eyed him suspiciously but, after a moment, seemed to accept his assertion, at least superficially. She took a step back, and he noticed that she was still wearing Malachi's oversized shirt, and nothing else.

"We go upstairs now." It was not a suggestion.

Irina led the way, taking the stairs gracefully, her long, porcelain legs stretching out in full upon every step.

But Dorian hardly noticed the sensual woman before him, even as the shirt rode up and the absence of her underwear became apparent.

He was too focussed upon that door. And the mysterious world that lay behind it.

5. Intrusion

"OH NO! OH no!"

Mick smacked the balloon away with a grin and turned to face the front door as it cracked open and, from behind it, a voice bellowed, "Let's get this bitch started!"

A moment later, Travis Street burst into the living room and spiked the balloon straight into a corner table, where it popped with a deafening crack, his shoulder-length, dirty blonde hair flying in the wind he created. "My point!" Travis pumped both fists while simultaneously flipping off both Mick and Gavin.

Behind him, his girlfriend, Alyssa, strode into the room, a small pink handbag that matched her hair slung over one shoulder and her face planted firmly in her palm. But over the tips of her fingers, her eyes smiled at her boyfriend's wild entry.

Travis flipped up on the couch and declared, "Happy birthday, bitch!" before throwing two handfuls of confetti at Kaylyn.

"You're going to break the couch," Kaylyn admonished while enjoying the spectacle.

"Then sit somewhere else," came Travis' dry reply before he fist-bumped Mallory and carried on to high-five everyone in the room.

"Fun trip up?" Gavin raised an eyebrow at Alyssa, who just shook her head.

"This is what happens when you bottle him up for three hours."

"Looks like his head might be about to pop off." Mick looked on to where Travis was now headbanging to the Latin trap Brady was playing on the house Bluetooth speaker.

"Oh no," Alyssa moaned, "he's going to rip his stitches. I'll be back." And she rushed off to protect the forehead that Travis had so recently crashed into a tree.

Shutting the front door behind him, Maverick Chow lugged three heavy bags, one of which was his own, into the front hall and deposited two of them carelessly. The third was laid down with love.

"What's up, Mav?" He and Gavin performed an awkward bro hug as Mick excused himself to chat with a nearly catatonic Brady.

"I think he's finally lost his mind," Mav mused of Travis in his standard high-pitched monotone.

"You just haven't known him long enough. That happened years ago."

Mav's eyes were still fixed on the wild man across the room, now trying to force Alyssa to dance with him. So self-confident it was hard to believe he was only twenty-three. "I have no idea how that guy serves guests on a nightly basis and hasn't gotten fired, yet."

"Could probably say the same thing about you." Gavin punched his friend lightly in the arm.

"But he's a server. I'm just a busboy. As long as I apologize when I throw food at the guests, no one notices me."

"Of course, you would apologize." Malachi slapped Mav on the shoulder. "You're a saint." Mav smiled innocently.

"You see the game last night?" Mav turned to Malachi.

"No, got it taped on my phone. Going to watch it tonight, if I can figure out how to work the thing."

"What's it like to be an old man?" Gavin asked.

"Hey, hey," Malachi cautioned. "Thirty is *not* old. Now, thirty-one, on the other hand…"

"I think that's when you have to learn hieroglyphics," Mav noted.

"Only three more months; I've already signed up for Rosetta Stone 101!"

Malachi and Gavin engaged in a deep discussion about the history of Egyptian politics as Mav slid uncomfortably to the background. The newest addition to the Asher's Palace team, he still hadn't solidified connections with everyone present. And while he'd formed strong friendships with Gavin, Kaylyn, Mallory, and Travis, handling himself around a larger group, where all four of his rocks could be occupied simultaneously, was still a struggle.

Just as he was beginning to fade into the background, he felt a tap on his shoulder and turned to see Kaylyn hovering beside him. "Hey, Mav!"

"Hey." He gave her a quick hug. "Happy almost birthday."

"Thanks! Have you seen my brother?"

Mav glanced to the door. "Him and his boyfriend were still outside when I came in. Taking pictures, I think."

Kaylyn rolled her eyes. "Influencers."

Mav added air quotes.

"True."

"What do they even influence?"

"No one. Fitness enthusiasts, in theory. Would be nice if they could at least come in and say 'hi', first, though. Not like the light's dying on them."

"I heard them say something about chiaroscuro and that's when I left them there."

They stood in silence for a minute, looking out upon the burgeoning party. "Sorry about your parents," Mav added, glancing over quickly but not wanting to make eye contact, at the same time.

Kaylyn shrugged. "Whatever. Forget it. This weekend is supposed to be fun." But she, too, averted her gaze. "Travis!" she cried out, suddenly. "Don't set off the smoke detector or we'll be asked to leave!" She rushed off to tend to the matter just as Irina crossed the room sharply, whispered something brusque into Malachi's ear, and dragged him into a corner, away from the party.

For a moment, Mav and Gavin watched on, slightly horrified, slightly bemused, as she berated Malachi for something or other, and he apologized profusely, though his face betrayed his uncertainty about what, precisely, he'd done wrong.

"She's crazy," Mav said.

"I think she's just uncomfortable around so many people she doesn't know that well…" Gavin attempted, but he couldn't quite convince himself.

"By the way…" Mav turned to Gavin and lowered his voice. As if by instinct, they both took a half step further away from the rest of the group. "How well do you know Kaylyn's brother?"

"Torri? Not that well. Met him a couple of times on trips and when we've gone out, but he's always seemed kinda quiet. Or, maybe *I* was too quiet. Whatever. Not well. Why?"

"I've never met him before today, so I don't know what he's usually like."

"What's that supposed to mean?"

Another half-step back. "It's just—I don't think he's taking the whole thing with their parents as well as Kaylyn is."

"I mean, that's kind of understandable, considering. Kaylyn can be…strong."

"Forced."

"She compartmentalizes."

"Well, I think Torri might compartmentalize, too. Just, with a little help." He snorted and wiped his nose before raising an eyebrow as if to say, *know what I mean?*

"Oh." Gavin went silent for a moment. "What—I don't know if you know and I've been scared to ask. Do you know what happened?"

This time, a full step back. "Just what Mallory told me. And, what Torri said in the car, today." He lowered his voice. "But, it sounds like it was a drive-by shooting. Completely random. Wrong place, wrong time, innocent bystanders."

"Damn. Any leads?"

"If what I've found online is true…"

"And who knows, really?"

"…it doesn't sound like it. They don't even know who the target actually was."

"Damn," Gavin repeated. "I don't know how either of them could possibly enjoy this weekend."

"One of them definitely won't."

Gavin went cold, at first from the mental image of the crime scene he had seen in an article he'd read three weeks ago, when it happened. Then, from icy condensation against the back of his neck. He turned, as did Mav, to face Travis, who was gleefully holding bottles of beer against their skin, fresh from the freezer.

"I know I just got here"—Travis looked from one to the other—"so maybe I don't know what the etiquette of this birthday *party* is supposed to be. But, WHY THE HELL AREN'T YOU TWO *DRINKING?*"

With his teeth, he popped each bottle cap and set the beers into his friends' hands. Grabbing his own from the kitchen counter, he tapped the tops of each bottle just as the foam began to overflow. "And listen: when I come back, I'd better see at least six empty bottles on that counter."

"Should you really be drinking on your meds?" Gavin indicated the gash on Travis' forehead.

"I don't friggin' care." Travis rolled his eyes and flitted away.

"Cheers," Gavin offered.

"More like, bottoms up." Mav began to chug.

6. Rest

ALCOHOL TURNED TO reckless and uncomfortable conversation, which turned to more alcohol, and, finally, to games.

And, though Kaylyn and Dorian were decidedly poor at beer pong, they had made a point of playing—and losing—as many games as they could. Gavin and Mav had taken them down in ten turns. Torri and Jim, finally in from the cold, had grudgingly agreed to play one quick, and successful, round before coming up with their captions. Even Mallory and Mick, forming a makeshift team of two acquaintances who barely knew each other, managed to sink all of their balls after fifty-two rounds, while Kaylyn and Dorian left four cups sitting on the table.

It was Travis and Alyssa's turn to face the reliable losers, and to their disappointment, they were not winning fast enough. "Hit the cup on the table, not on her boob!" Travis exclaimed after Alyssa took a particularly poor shot off Kaylyn's chest.

From the spectator's gallery in swivel stools, Gavin laughed and Mallory rolled her eyes. Alyssa ignored him, as was familiar by this point.

"Air ball," Dorian said, leading Travis to whip his ping pong ball into enemy territory.

The frustration was misplaced, however, as Kaylyn quickly air balled, herself, sending the game back into Travis and Alyssa's court.

With a deep breath and anger in his eyes, Travis lined up the perfect shot with one, two, three pumps of the wrist.

"Watch the elbows," Mallory chided as Travis' arm crept over the table, swigging back the final dregs of her gin and tonic before grimacing and pouring herself another.

"You know what"—Travis pointed at her—"for someone with chicken elbows, you're not really one to talk about what mine do."

Mallory casually flipped him off as she took another drink.

"Hey, hey, come on." Gavin smirked, six beers deep and numb to reality. "We all know Travis is always a cheater."

For a brief moment, the humour drained from Travis' face and he stared coldly at Gavin, who bit his lip and averted eye contact as he swilled down the final dregs of his drink.

"It's okay." Alyssa laid a hand on Travis' shoulder and looked up at him with her deep cerulean eyes, which seemed to case him in the calm of the sea. "You can do this from a step further back."

Travis relaxed immediately, his shoulders dropping, tongue detaching itself from the roof of his mouth. He took a deep breath and blinked slowly. She calmed him. She always calmed him, and though the time wasn't right to thank her for it, he still let the tips of his fingers draw gently along the flowing, mesh sleeve of her blouse before he took a step back and aimed.

In a moment, he'd sunk his ball and Alyssa had sunk hers in the same cup. "Three cups, balls back," Travis announced with a smile, immediately ready to throw again.

*

THE FIRE HAD taken a long time to get going—not helped by fingers frozen to immobility after the long and arduous trek down to the firepit—and it survived mostly on the twigs that Mav scavenged from the base of trees. Malachi had suggested getting the fire going, if for no other reason than to escape the demands that awaited him in the house, and Mav had been happy enough to get away from the uncomfortable milling about.

As for Mick, he had just tagged along, as he had done, often, throughout his life. At a young age, Mick had learned that no one could be counted upon to follow him. Not his best friend, Donny, who'd tossed him aside in favour of James, the so-called 'bad kid'. Not his brother Sammy, who'd always found time to play with him until he'd turned fourteen and had better things to do, and better people to hang out with, than his eight-year-old brother. Certainly not his parents, who spent more time chasing each other around with wooden spoons and closed fists to notice, particularly, what forgotten Mick Martin had on his childish mind.

So, Mick had become a follower. If it seemed like a good time, he was there, and ready to contribute. If it had the mildest form of potential, he would be there to help bring it to its peak.

Always a giver and rarely a taker, Mick went not to suckle from the teat of pleasure, but to bring his own milk to the party. And, even if it meant hanging out with babies, it was preferable to the solitude of his past.

"You know," Mick started in his drole monotone, talking loudly to drown out the ominous rush of the lake below, "if it runs down, I'm pretty sure I saw an axe in the garage. We could always cut down one of these trees."

"I think I'll just go back inside if it gets to that point," Mav said.

Malachi gestured around to the various trees. "It really only makes sense if there's a good tree around here. Now, there are a lot of maple trees around, which isn't a bad choice, but it's dark out here, and there are a lot of elms around, as well. Elms: not such a great choice."

"If we keep talking about trees, I might just jump into the fire."

"Well," Malachi hummed, "that's a different kind of wood, altogether."

"Only when you're around." He made a quick kiss face at Malachi, who chortled before shaking his head.

"It would be wrong to think of you like that, Mav. You're too much of a saint."

"All right, then." Mick clapped his knees definitively and checked his watch: quarter-to-ten. "Sounds

like you two could use a little privacy and I meant to
go to bed an hour ago."

"It's so early," Mav noted.

"Up since five-thirty."

"It's so early!" Mav repeated.

"I'll see you guys in the morning." Mick stood
and stretched his legs, feeling more fire burning
through them for having sat in the cold for so long
than he'd felt from the fire, itself.

He stepped forward to warm his hands one last
time, just as the fire spurted up, sending him stumbling backward into a half-seated position.

And rising up above him, the fire seemed to lick
forward, threatening to engulf him. Deep, in the darkest orange of the flame's centre, a white flicker
blinded him. He squinted more closely, trying to
make out a feature of the wispy spectacle. Five lines,
meeting a ball and…

…it was a hand. A skeletal hand climbing from
the centre of the fire, Mick would've sworn it.
Lengthening and reaching out. An arm, a shoulder,
and then…

…the flame lowered as quickly as it had ignited.

"Careful, there!" Malachi warned good-naturedly,
blissfully unaware of the spectre that had appeared
before Mick's eyes.

He shook his head. Fatigue and alcohol: a bad
combination.

Mick waved without looking as he walked past
them and toward the house, remembering just in time
that he would need to go around the side to the front
as the back patio was unsafe. As the fire faded further

and further into the distance, and his eyes failed to adjust to the dark, he was plunged into the blackness of the night, feeling his way slowly up the stony steps and across the weeds that threatened to trip him at every step.

An owl cawed in the distance—no, that couldn't have been right. Hooted.

But it hadn't hooted. It had cawed.

Mick hurried his pace, stumbling forward partly from his imbibed lack of balance and partly from the long and stringy weeds, the loose shoelaces of nature.

He crashed into a tree along the property line and felt his way to the next, hand wet and sticky with sap and dew.

He had to be next to the house now—he was sure of it. The darkness to his left seemed even darker than before. Closing his eyes—it really didn't make much of a difference—he pressed forward faster, trying to focus on staying upright, but disappearing further into the abyss.

In the distance, a tiny flicker gave him hope. The single streetlight along Spruce Road guided him back to safety and, when he saw it, he ran.

Ran to the road, ran to the door, ran to the stairs, and ran to the basement. And not a soul, in their preoccupation and inebriation, noticed that he had come and gone.

In the dark of the basement, Mick fumbled for a light switch, completely unaware of where it might be. He tripped over a corner table and cursed loudly, the bang ringing in his ears as the pain rang in his shin.

He pushed his way to the edge of the room, to where he was sure the bathroom lay, and shoved the door open.

From the sink, a pale, white Torri Singh turned to face him, his eyes sunken black, the whites taking up almost his entire eyeball. Mick backed away slowly as Kaylyn's brother absently, hollowly, wiped away his powder moustache. He barely seemed to move as the door shut before him and Mick was left in darkness once again, just a sliver of light gleaming in a halo around the door.

Behind him, a loud, echoing bang, as if metal were being crushed, rang out through the room, but the echo did not finish, as though the sound had been eaten halfway through the note. He whipped around to face an empty room, his eyes starting to adjust to the darkness. Nothing seemed out of place. No one moved.

The sound rang out again, drawing the hairs up on his arms. Mick followed the noise to the locked door at the side of the room. He waited, wondering if it would bang again.

Nothing. Silence. The cold crept further into the room.

Rubbing his hand to keep the skin from cracking, he gripped the handle and turned. Futile. It would not budge.

The boiler. It had to have been the boiler, he told himself, though he had no idea what a boiler should sound like, aside from the fact that it shouldn't have been that.

Turning, Mick raced toward his bedroom, no longer feeling the need to brush his teeth before collapsing.

There was no time to turn the lights on. Certainly, no time to get changed. He threw himself into the bed before him and drew the blankets over his face. Breathing heavily, and desperately wishing that Brady were there, Mick closed his eyes and begged for morning.

He would not fall asleep; he could not fall asleep. Not with what he had seen, heard. His heart was pounding through the walls of his chest and his mouth was drier than his throat.

But between alcohol and fatigue, even the protective urge to stay alert can fade, and Mick was asleep in minutes, dead to the world, and unaware of what would happen next.

7. Party

"WE'RE DONE," KAYLYN declared.

"Winner's table anyway," Travis noted, re-racking his and Alyssa's cups.

"I got next game." Brady stumbled to his feet, butting out his cigarette dangerously close to the fire detector and lurching toward the table to displace Dorian, who'd slid away the moment the pathetic game had ended.

"Who're you playing with though?"

Brady scanned the room and found most engaged or absent. He hesitated a moment. A minute. Two. "Um…" He drew a pointed finger around at everyone before settling upon "Gavin?"

"I'm with Mav."

"It's fine," Brady encouraged, but Gavin shook his head.

"Gotta stay loyal to my partner."

Brady bit the inside of his cheek. "What happened to Mick?"

"Think he went to bed," Dorian called over his shoulder as he arrived back upstairs, now walking toward the bedrooms.

"What about you?" Brady brandished a ball in Dorian's direction.

"Also going to bed," he replied, not turning around this time. "Long drive. 'Night everyone." Though no one wished it back at him.

Brady blindly chucked the ball in the direction of Travis' cups, probably not realizing that he sunk it. "Does anyone not have a partner?"

Gavin checked around the room before whispering, "Irina, I think. Malachi probably wouldn't care."

Brady blinked. "Anyone else?"

"Did I hear my name?" Irina approached sternly, as though to mention her was her personal copyright.

"You're Brady's partner for beer pong," Gavin declared, alcohol granting him the confidence to eschew requests.

Irina stared at Brady for a minute before deciding. "No."

"Come on," Gavin pled. "You're the only one inside without a partner."

"I do not know this game and I do not care to."

"You're not going to have to play it for long." Travis lined up as if to shoot.

After a moment and a disgruntled breath, Irina pursed her lips. "Fine. But you—" She jabbed Brady in the chest with a black false fingernail. "You make it so I do not do the naked run."

"We're not playing with that rule," Alyssa offered with a smile that got shot down quickly by a glare.

Meanwhile, Travis muttered, "Kinda are," but he didn't dare say it loudly enough to be heard.

Irina lined up and, for someone who claimed not to know the rules, played as though she did. On her first attempt, she sunk a ball and on her second, she whipped the ball so hard that it knocked a cup off the table, altogether.

"Whoa, settle down," Brady said with a half-laugh.

"We win point, we win game," Irina replied mechanically.

"You could try not to get us wet in the process," Travis complained, shaking out a sopping sock, violently.

"You do not complain when you win; you should not complain when you lose."

Travis and Alyssa missed their shots and Irina immediately fired back another vicious ball that knocked one cup into another, sending both over and onto Alyssa's jeans. The rest of the match went in much the same manner, with Irina emerging, and retiring, victorious, while Brady politely accepted his role in the bloodbath.

"I'm going downstairs to change." Alyssa looked up at Travis sheepishly, the water splatter causing her to look as though she'd wet her pants.

"Do you mind…?" Travis extended his soaking socks for her to take down with her. As she headed downstairs, Travis moved to the kitchen to grab some paper towel and wipe off the rest of his loss's memory.

"Have you told her?" Kaylyn appeared at his side with a sharply raised eyebrow.

Travis stared at her for a moment, dropping his voice. "I told you," he began. "I'm not telling her."

"But you're going to stop."

"Yes. *Yes*, I'm going to stop. I promised you that."

Kaylyn clenched her teeth. "'Cause, you know—it makes me *so* mad, honestly…"

"I know, I know. We see things differently, okay. But I'm doing this for you, because your friendship is more important to me."

"Than what?" Alyssa appeared at Kaylyn's shoulder, now wearing Travis' sweatpants, brushing a long, pink lock of hair from her eyes.

"Than winning some stupid game of beer pong," Travis recovered quickly, though he still hit Kaylyn with a brief glare for her timing and location for this conversation.

"Aw." Alyssa made a mock 'how sweet' expression. "You finally got him to admit that winning isn't everything."

"I didn't say that."

But Alyssa shook her head. "You've changed. You're so soft now."

"Take it back." She ran as he chased after her playfully. "Take it back!"

"You're like a teddy bear," she called over her shoulder, hair flying out behind her as she leapt over a couch and landed, seated, next to Brady.

Butting out his spliff, Brady opened his eyes widely at the intrusion of his visitor and gave her a quick once-over, taking in her svelte physique, hourglass figure, innocently freckled face. "Well, hello there." He leant his head against his hand and his elbow against the couch back. "And what can I thank for this pleasure?"

Before she could reply, she was interrupted by the slam of the front door and a loud cry of, "We go to bed. Now!" Irina stormed across the living room to where Malachi and Mav had finally come in from dousing the fire. She grabbed Malachi's arm and he looked around uselessly, as if for help he knew he could not receive. With a defeated shrug, he allowed her to yank his three-hundred-pound frame to the stairwell and out of sight, with one last look to the party he would so sorely miss.

"Daaaamn." Brady whistled. "I'd never treat my woman the way he lets her treat him." He pointed a lazy finger gun at Alyssa. "And you feel free to check that out, any time."

From behind him, a throat cleared, and Brady looked up to see Travis, normally a few inches shorter than he, now towering over him, his long blonde hair silhouetted in the light, making his head appear twice its normal size. "I'm pretty sure she's not interested in someone as ugly as you, bud," Travis jabbed, and Brady just laughed.

Travis slid over the back of the couch and landed between Brady and Alyssa.

"You two a thing?" Brady pointed from one to the other, obliviously.

"More than just any thing; we're gold, and not in the market for silver."

Brady shook his head with another smile.

"Stop it," Alyssa whispered meekly in Travis' ear, pouting.

"Didn't they tell you not to show up high for the interview?"

"Come on," Alyssa pleaded, though not entirely seriously, as she yanked Travis' arm away.

Brady offered them a mock salute as they crossed to the opposite side of the room. "Calm down; it's not a big deal," Alyssa soothed as they neared he staircase.

"Oh, come on." Travis brushed it off. "I'm not really mad." But something in his eyes, in the way he looked back at Brady with a 'mock' snarl, left her unconvinced. She laid a hand on his face and pulled his eyes toward her.

"Let him hit on me. It's not like I'd leave you for him. And, it makes me feel pretty." Although, really, it irritated her, no end.

"You don't need his attention to know you're pretty. Besides, you're not just pretty. You're the hottest person in this room, and probably in the country."

"I love you." She kissed him gently.

"I'd kill for you, you know that?"

"I know." And she kissed him again.

He was gazing deeply into her cerulean eyes when he felt a hand grab his shoulder and pivot him toward the centre of the room. Torri, Kaylyn's brother, deposited a phone into his hand and led his boyfriend, Jim, into the heart of the party.

"We need party pics for social," Torri declared, pulling up the collar on his workout attire. Jim slightly lowered the zipper on his tracksuit-esque ensemble.

"You don't look like you're here to have fun," Travis noted, snapping a few useless candids and trying, futilely, to hand the phone back.

"Need to keep up images."

The piney aroma he noted as his attempt to escape their snare was rebuffed confirmed that, in spite of their attire, they were showered and coiffed for the occasion.

They posed with balloons, threw streamers in the air, took down half the hard work Kaylyn had put into setting up the atmosphere for the sake of 'better lighting' or 'complementary colours'. Travis glanced back at Alyssa after every set of pointless shots, her eyes calling him closer as she backed toward the stairs.

He was barely looking as he snapped his pictures and asked, uselessly, "Good enough?"

"If you need to ask"—Jim looked down his pointed nose at him—"then the answer is no."

Travis grinned at Kaylyn, rolling her eyes on the other side of the room, watching on disapprovingly as her brother stole the show.

Finally giving up, Travis took a few more shots, noting, "You look terrible in that one"; "Definitely don't post that"; "You're gonna lose followers no matter which of these you use"; "Try facing away from the camera…yeah, no one needs to see your faces…actually, your asses aren't any better."

"Can you take this seriously, *please*?" Torri admonished, though his gaze was more glazed than angry. "We don't come to your job and mess it up."

"No, you just come to our party and mess it up," Travis murmured, wanting to say it louder but not wanting Kaylyn to hear. After all, while Torri and Jim may not have been part of the Palace staff, Kaylyn made a point of inviting them to all events, and insulting them too loudly would have made it more likely that he would be cut from the group than the irritants.

He took a few more pictures before he saw Alyssa mouth the words, "Come on," while toying at the frilly lace just below her neck.

"That one's fine," he announced, putting the phone down on a side table and heading for his girlfriend.

"Hey!" Torri called, recovering the phone. "We're not done yet!"

"That sounds like a you problem," Travis called back, taking Alyssa's hips and guiding her down the stairs before him.

"Ready for bed?" Alyssa whispered in his ear.

Without a word, Travis kissed the back of her neck and rushed her into their bedroom, just to the left of the staircase.

Pulling the door tightly behind him, he had his shirt half off and his hard six-pack abs out before Alyssa had a chance to turn around. She stepped forward to run a fingernail up and down his bare skin while he gently slipped his fingers beneath the back of her blouse and ran his hands up her smooth back.

He tucked his lips between hers as she licked a coquettish tongue across his teeth. Then, with a not-so-gentle shove, he knocked her back, toward the bed, where she fell with a laugh, as he dropped down on top of her and kissed the side of her neck.

"I love you," she whispered as he curled her pink hair around his fingertips. She focussed on his lips, kissing deeply, violently, biting his lower lip to the brink of blood, while his hand took hers and squeezed firmly.

Grabbing at Travis' powerful shoulders, Alyssa flipped him onto his back and held his chest down, teasing him with fluid touches.

Travis grabbed for her shoulders and massaged them gently as she smiled sweetly down at him. He looked up to her long neck and leaned upward to kiss it, once more.

But stopped.

Because, somewhere in the corner of the room, he saw a flash of blackness. As if someone were watching. He turned his head, but the image was gone. Alyssa didn't seem to notice. Shaking his head, he closed his eyes and tried to recapture the moment. But, when he opened them again, the darkness was closer. A shadow in the middle of the room, but much too thick to be a shadow.

"Wait!" he tried to say, but his mouth opened dryly and Alyssa kissed him hard, shutting his voice inside.

She shifted her long, pink hair out of his eyes and the thing seemed to be right behind her, now, dark yet translucent, grasping forward for her neck.

Cold and ridden with instinctive terror, he reached up toward the darkness, to bat it away. And just as his fingers came an inch from contact, a crash resounded from upstairs, followed by a scream.

And the shadow was gone.

8. Collapse

ALYSSA FELL OFF of him and rolled onto the bed, subconsciously adjusting the bottom of her blouse. "What was that?"

"I don't know," Travis managed weakly, dragging himself to the edge of the bed and pulling his shirt back on. "I'll be right back…" He considered for a second before calling back over his shoulder, "…Stay here and don't let anyone in."

Slightly confused but all-too-happy to remain in place, Alyssa cuddled up tightly under the sheets and watched the closed door attentively.

Travis raced up the stairs, sweating, heart racing.

In the centre of the living room, a full group of the awake members of the party stood in an ominous circle, looking down upon something hidden within their midst.

Gavin bore an expression of shock, Jim one of horror.

Travis pushed forward, knocking his way past Mallory, who barely noticed that she was being moved until she was already out of the path.

"What happened?" Travis asked breathlessly.

He looked down upon the centre of the circle, where Torri lay in a crumpled heap, unconscious.

For a moment, Travis wasn't sure whether or not the man was breathing. He seemed so still, so cold. And then he heaved forward and vomited, loudly spewing orange detritus from deep within his guts. And it wouldn't stop.

Jim rushed forward to hold Torri's head, his long hair, to tell him that he was going to be all right, but he certainly didn't look all right. The rancid odor of sick permeated the room, leading Gavin to take a step backward and Brady to dry-retch, turning around to try to avoid the disgusting sight.

"It's okay, it's okay," Jim murmured softly, rubbing Torri's back. "Get it all out. Better now than in the morning."

"They were going around taking pictures—or *trying* to get people to take pictures of them, anyway," Mallory explained, "and then Torri just collapsed out of nowhere."

"He's on something," Mav noted emotionlessly, glancing over quickly at Travis, meeting his eyes for a knowing moment.

"He's drunk. That's all," Jim stated forcefully. "He's been drinking all night and just had too much. Like probably the rest of you will realize you have by the morning." He was almost accusatory now, protecting Torri so desperately that he was impossible to believe.

"We should call the hospital," Kaylyn suggested, although her face betrayed a tear between concern and suspicion, underlined with frustration.

"No!" Jim snarled. "He doesn't need a hospital. He needs sleep and water. Someone get him a glass of water."

Obediently, Gavin rushed for the tap, struggling to find a clean glass in the process.

Torri breathed heavily upon the floor, sweat beads bursting from his forehead and dripping toward his eyebrows. "It's okay," Jim whispered, "you're almost done. You're almost fine." But the glazed, dazed look of Torri's rolled-back eyes looked far from 'fine'.

Travis stepped forward and took a knee. "Can you see my finger?" He held up one finger before the fallen man, drawing it left to right. His pupils did not follow.

Jim slapped his hand away. "Give him a minute. How'd you like someone sticking a finger in your face when you don't feel well?"

"Probably better than being left for dead from improper treatment," Travis muttered.

"What was that?" Jim turned on him fierily.

"Nothing," he grunted. "Let's just get him to bed, all right?"

Grabbing one arm, while Jim took the other, they hoisted Torri upright and held the entirety of his weight. His legs would not straighten.

"Last chance to sit him down and call an ambulance."

"Can't call an ambulance anyway," Mav said. "No service out here."

"All right, then, let's go." Travis stepped forward and Torri immediately vomited again, this time sending warm, foul-odoured liquid across Travis' foot.

He gritted his teeth and tried to ignore the sensation, but he kept the majority of his foot off the ground with each step.

Together, they managed to deposit Torri into his bed and turn him on his side—a task he made as difficult as possible, back arched constantly in all the wrong directions.

"I got him." Jim ran a hand through Torri's hair. "Pass me a bucket." Travis grabbed the garbage can from the bathroom and slid it along the floor to him, returning to the main area, once again.

"I can't believe this." Kaylyn held her face in her palm. "On *my* birthday weekend. He had to go and do this. Oh, my God!"

Gritting her teeth and glancing at the bedroom door, Mallory tried to find a way to disagree, to protect the sickly brother. But she couldn't bring herself to oppose her friend, and finally settled on, "Yeah, totally," with accompanying eye roll.

"I think it might be time that we all go to bed," Gavin prompted softly and no one responded. But Gavin was used to being ignored, and equally used to others following his plans without a word of acknowledgement.

Everyone stood still for a few moments longer, considering the scene, glancing toward the bedroom door. And, finally, they all went their separate ways, to change and brush their teeth, and to leave the rest of the party for the morning.

9. Night

THE BASEMENT WAS too quiet. Gavin shut his eyes tightly in the bed between Mav's and Mallory's, but no matter what level of shut he chose, they always felt a little too loose. He reached up and rubbed them, trying to instill some sense of fatigue into his face that would hopefully spread to the rest of his body. *Maybe I should read a book*, he thought, seeking anything that might tire him out. But that would involve opening his eyes for more than a minute or two, and something about the air in The Little Maple Cabin on Spruce Road suggested that that was worse than a little lost sleep.

He turned onto his side, then the other. Pulled the sheets up over his head. The pillow. He could read under the covers, off of his phone.

But his phone was down to five percent battery life and the outlet was across the room, by the door.

Okay, he thought. *I'm going to open my eyes. I'm going to open my eyes to remind my brain that it's dark out and it's time for bed and to tell it to stop worrying because everything is fine. And there are no ghosts in this house.*

That was a mistake. He shouldn't have let himself think about it—about *them*—so explicitly. His heart skipped at the sound of a creak from the house's foundation.

With a hard swallow, he opened his eyes and felt no change in his level of fatigue. "Come on," he whine-whispered to himself.

Everyone else was asleep—it was as though they'd passed out the moment that they hit their pillows. And, simply, it wasn't fair.

He glanced over at Mallory, chest rising and falling slowly in the tiny sliver of moonlight that fought its way through the window.

Then he switched his gaze over to Mav, rolling and turning in the fit of a dream. How fortunate they were to have been courted by sleep.

Gavin rubbed his eyelids, once again. He'd had trouble sleeping as a child, but hadn't recently. With time, he'd learned to relax, if only while lying down. The rest of the time, he would still be his standard bundle of nerves. But the nights were his own, a time for shutting off the world and seeking respite in sleep.

Tonight, however, he was overcome. Not even the eight or ten drinks he'd poured down his throat, which normally would have had him near passing out in the middle of a conversation, seemed to have any effect. The haze of drunkenness had started to wane and he felt strangely lucid.

He tried to turn his thoughts to happier things: his mother's meatloaf; his father's prize-winning garden; his girlfriend's eyes, nose, mouth. He imagined her next to him, providing a comforting hug that he could cuddle into. His eyes started to close again and he felt it coming—rest, at least, if not sleep. The calm was only a step away from a passport to morning.

And just as he felt himself start to fade, to find solace even in the perturbing quiet of the middle of nowhere, he heard a scream.

It was quiet, muffled, but the closer he listened, the longer it persisted.

Then it stopped.

The boiler. It had to have been the boiler! But he couldn't convince himself. Because, if it was the boiler, it was the most human boiler he'd ever encountered.

The voice cried out, once again. A woman's, deep but feminine. Not like the voices of anyone he knew, though it was so hard to tell with a scream.

Gavin felt sweat slither down his palms. It sounded as though the voice were trying to say something, but he couldn't make out the words.

Shaking and suddenly very, very cold, Gavin forced himself up in the bed, breathing in staccato.

The scream paused again. This was his only chance and he forced the voice to his lips. "Mav? Mallory?" he whisper-called to them. They made no response. "Mav? Mallory?" he tried, a little bit louder this time.

Mallory snored and Mav turned over once more, but neither acknowledged him.

The moon was gone behind a cloud, now, and the room was almost completely dark. With a dry swallow, Gavin pushed himself off the edge of the bed and felt the cold chill of the floor shoot up violently through his bare feet.

And, at that very moment, the cry rang out again, slightly louder this time, the note cut every few moments as though it was weeping. Desperate and weeping.

"Mav?" He tried again, louder, hoping to drown out the distant voice. "Please? Wake up!" He shuffled across the floor and grabbed for Mav's shoulder, shaking him gently, then a little harder.

Mav rolled onto his back, mouth wide but eyes still shut.

"Mav? Do you hear that? Wake up."

The voice stopped and all was silent for a moment.

Mav's eyes shot open wide. He gasped at the air wheezingly, gaze fixed straight ahead upon the ceiling, but unseeing. In a clipped and raspy voice, completely unfamiliar from his standard high monotone, he cried out: "No! Manny, please! Please, Manny, let me go!"

Gavin leapt back and stumbled to the edge of his bed, smashing his calf hard against the bedframe but unable to call forth a scream of pain.

Mav remained frozen in bed, back arched upward, paralyzed. Then, he collapsed back down into the sheets, eyes shut, breathing the calm breaths of sleep, and returned to his dreaming.

It took Gavin a few minutes to realize that he was shaking and a few minutes more to regain enough control of his body to stand up again. By then, the pain in his leg was more of a dull reminder of a few moments past, and he stretched it out unconsciously as he stutter-walked to the closed door that led to the rest of the basement. Did he dare open it?

He had nearly decided against, reconsidering the semi-warmth of his bed and the hope that all of this would fade into distant memory by the morning. But, another scream froze him in place.

Swallowing hard, he looked back at the room, barely believing that they couldn't hear it. It was louder now, loud enough to render it hard to write off as his imagination.

He turned the door handle, but his sweaty palm slipped off it. He tried again, this time wrapping his hand in his sleeve. Then, he plunged himself into the pitch black of the empty basement.

The sound stopped almost immediately upon his exit from the bedroom, but not before he had identified the general location from which it had come. The door with 'nothing' behind it. He didn't know where the light switches were, but was fairly confident they were on the other side of the room. And he'd forgotten to bring his phone and its flashlight with him. Knowing that if he turned back to get it, he would never make this trek, and would be left wondering for the rest of the night, he began his approach slowly, in complete darkness.

The floor creaked as he stepped slowly toward the door, seeming to echo throughout the massive room. As he neared the wall, he reached out to get his bearings. It was farther away than he expected and he explored into nothingness, feeling as if the world had fallen away around him. His slow shuffle steps ground loudly in his ears, and his heartbeat provided an achingly rapid metronome to his every movement.

His fingertips made cold contact with the wooden panelling of the wall and a sense near to relief shot through him, though it did not last long at the memory of his task. He pressed himself against the wall as he tried to feel his way toward the door. The space between boards pinched at his fingers.

He was a few feet away when he heard a soft, feminine voice in his ear: "Hey."

He jumped and turned, smacking the back of his head against the wall, which sent him tumbling groundward.

Knees buckled and back barely propped up against the wall, he stared up into a blinding light, the figure before him halfway between angelic in the garish yellow, and devilish in the vast darkness that surrounded her.

She leaned down close and Gavin tried to push himself away, but his weak, scrawny arms gave out on him and he plummeted further to the floor.

"Gavin, it's okay." Alyssa shifted her cellphone flashlight to the side, slightly, and revealed her living face.

"It's you. Okay, okay." He tried to catch his breath, momentarily forgetting the screams that had drawn him to this place.

"What are you doing out here?" she whispered.

"I…" He hesitated, suddenly afraid to sound stupid. "I…thought I heard something."

Her face went blank and cold. "I thought I was going crazy."

"You heard it, too?"

"It was saying something. *She* was saying something," Alyssa absently reached down to help Gavin back up. "I don't know what, though."

Gavin rubbed the back of his head gingerly. "Do you think…?" He swallowed and bit his lip. "Do you think there's any chance she might've been saying, 'No! Manny, please! Please, Manny, let me go?'"

Alyssa pursed her thin, fragile lips. "It could've been…is that what you heard?"

"No. Something Mav said in a dream. Or maybe…no, no, it was a dream."

"Where do you think it was coming from?"

He gestured to the locked door, now shadowed, but visible, in the aura of her light.

"I'm pretty sure it's locked," Alyssa noted, a half-attempt at escaping what they knew they had to do.

Gavin said nothing. He let the last bit of adrenaline left in his system carry him to the door. Wrapping his fingers shakingly about the handle, he turned and yanked. Then yanked again. "Still locked."

Alyssa licked dry lips with a dry tongue. "Call out to her. If someone's locked in there, we need to know."

Gavin rapped softly on the door. "Hello?" He pressed his ear to the wood and listened. Nothing. "Hello?" he offered, louder. Again, nothing. "Is someone in there?"

They waited, waited. Time stopped and raced simultaneously, but the scream did not return, nor any other response. Gavin turned, shaking his head. "I don't think there's…"

But he could not finish the sentence. In the furthest corner of the room, past Alyssa's left shoulder, he saw something move. He blinked, the dark shadow racing into the darkness and gone.

His mouth hung open as the figure swept back into the light, moving slowly now, creeping up behind Alyssa, reaching out, reaching for her neck.

"Watch out!" he cried, pointing in the direction of the featureless figure.

Alyssa whipped around, shining her flashlight all about the room. But nothing was there.

"What was that about?" She turned back to Gavin, eyes wide with fear but equal part confused.

"There was, it was…" He shook his head, seeking the figure in the darkness, yet again, but finding nothing. "Must've been a trick of the light."

As if called upon from the Heavens, the light flicked on in that very moment, blinding them both.

Covering their eyes and instinctively backing up toward the wall, ready to fight but wanting to run, they blinked themselves back to the present to find a figure glaring at them from the other side of the room.

Irina, hair dishevelled, glowered at them with more death in her dark black falcon eyes than any ghost could have threatened.

"Why do you make such loud noise? If you want to have affair, do with action, not words."

"We're not…" Gavin started.

"I do not care what it is you are doing. But you will do it quietly!" she yelled. "Go to bed!"

She flicked the light off again and disappeared back into her room. In the low illumination of Alyssa's still-lit flashlight, they shared a grimace.

"Let's pretend this never happened?" Alyssa suggested.

"Agreed." Gavin started back toward his room, pausing with his hand on the handle. Turning back to Alyssa, now in nearly the same pose at her own door, he whispered, "What *did* happen?"

She shook her head. "Nothing." And without turning to look back at him, she entered her bedroom and plunged the basement back into darkness.

10. Morning

WHEN GAVIN AWOKE to the sun blazing through the window above his head, he felt no safer than he had in the dark.

He was soaked in sweat and his throat cracked as he tried to swallow in the cold. Glancing to his left, he found that Mav was long gone, bed made up as though he'd never been there. Mallory still slept to his right, mouth hanging open, glasses glinting in the sunlight on her nightstand.

Checking his phone—now at three percent—he found it to be one in the afternoon and couldn't believe he'd slept that long while still feeling so dreadfully exhausted.

The alcohol had worked its way to his brain, and a shooting headache screamed at him either to close his eyes again or go get a glass of water.

And while the temptation to waste the day away, hidden beneath the safety of his covers seemed appealing, the thought of being the last one left in this room when Mallory awoke spurred him to action and sent him racing for his toothbrush. In the main basement room, he turned away from and rushed past the locked door, imagining that, if he couldn't see it, it didn't exist.

He prepared for the day as quickly as he could, suffering through a cold shower and the quickest brush his sensitive teeth could handle. Never had he taken stairs so quickly in his life.

In the kitchen, Brady vaped cannabis without a care in the world, leaning back precariously on his barstool by the kitchen island. In the kitchen, Kaylyn was busy chopping—her fingers in constant peril from her questionable knife form—and Jim washed lettuce in the sink. "What's lunch?" Gavin asked, swinging himself into the seat next to Brady, sucking in a waft of smoke, having a nasty flashback to the car ride up, and shifting to the next seat down.

"Poison," Jim grunted.

"Creamy Alfredo pasta," Kaylyn replied with an angry glare at Jim while she continued to slice.

"The amount of butter, oil, and cheese you put into this thing is enough to make all of us sick ten times over," Jim contested.

"You know what?" Kaylyn turned to face Jim, knife still in hand. "You eat healthy three hundred and sixty plus days a year. You can eat what I want for a couple of meals for *my birthday weekend!*"

Jim stared her down, unfazed by the weapon between them. Finally, he declared, "Torri and I will be having the salad," and resumed fixing his private meal.

"How's Torri doing?" Gavin inquired, glancing back at the shut door to his bedroom.

"He's fine," Jim replied, a little too quickly. "Just a bit hungover. Headache. He'll be out in a bit."

He was sufficiently defensive that it didn't feel wise to push the matter any further. "What about everyone else? Where are they?"

"Dorian took Mav, Malachi, and Irina to get a pie," Kaylyn started, "and a gift—that I'm not supposed to know about, by the way. And the others are still asleep." Kaylyn pursed her lips, clearly displeased to be alone for so long on her birthday trip.

"Surprised that Mick would still be out. He went to bed before the rest of us."

Brady chuckled. "Didn't hear jack from him all night or this morning. Didn't even snore. Boy's got 'sleeping issues.'"

"Yeah," Gavin said, "he was telling me."

The front door clicked open and the store quartet returned, not even bothering to hide their secret gift: a bottle of gin that Mav dropped triumphantly on the counter, though he coupled it with a chagrinned expression.

Irina stormed through in a huff, seemingly for no other reason than to ensure that everyone was aware of her huff, before heading back downstairs, Malachi in tow, the apologetic expression that seemed now permanently etched upon his face in full force.

On the way by, she nearly bowled over Travis and Alyssa, just making their way upstairs. They pressed hard up against the wall, flattened by the boiling breeze of her wrath.

"What in the hell happened out there?" Kaylyn demanded, dropping her knife.

"Looks like someone's upgraded to double-bitch mode this morning." Travis smirked, pulling back a stool for Alyssa before taking one, himself.

Dorian stepped into the kitchen, eyes sparkling a little more than the situation seemed to call for, but such was his way. He tossed his keys casually onto the island and leaned against it with both hands. "Had a bit of a debate over the gift. Irina said we should do something fancier than gin and that we were being bad friends; we told her it was Kaylyn's favourite but she didn't care. Kept putting it back and cursing at us in Russian." He paused. "Well, I assume, anyway." He thought for a second. "Oh, and, apparently, she's allergic to blueberries and said we should get a different pie, even though Kaylyn specifically asked for blueberry. But I don't know if that was true. I think she was just grumpy at that point and trying to be difficult."

"So you *do* eat fruit," Jim muttered under his breath.

"Anyway, long story short," Dorian continued, "Mav kinda snapped and got in her face and she didn't take that too well. Pretty sure she tried to slug him, but Malachi held her back. Then, Mav told her to go sit in the car until we were done and walked her right out the door."

"Seriously?" Travis leaned forward with a shocked smile. "Little Mavvy, all grown up, getting into a fight?"

"But he's such a saint," Gavin said. Mav didn't smile innocently this time.

"She pissed me off."

Coming from the most unassuming member of the group, no one was quite sure what to say. They were saved, instead, by Torri's bedroom door opening, and a glazed—but decidedly alive—man exiting, clad fully in workout attire and with two mats under his arms.

"How you feeling, Torri?" Kaylyn asked cursorily, but she couldn't look up to make eye contact with her brother.

"Fine," he offered, distantly. "I want to go outside to work out before it storms."

Instinctively, everyone looked out to the bright blue sky, hanging happily over the porch. But a quick turn of the head to the front window revealed a different story. Distant, grey clouds hovered ominously over the future.

"Don't you think you should rest?" Kaylyn's eyes narrowed, but Torri wasn't listening.

"You coming?" He gestured to Jim, who immediately dropped the lettuce in favour of a good, healthy workout.

"Are you serious?" Kaylyn demanded, frustratedly.

"It's sixty degrees out in the middle of November. I'm not wasting a chance for my last outdoor workout of the year." He didn't even look back as he joined his boyfriend on the way to the porch.

"Not that door," Brady reminded them in a moment of surprise lucidity and reaction time. Their eyes turned to the warning sign and a moment later they'd turned on their respective heels and headed for the front exit.

"Okay, cool, whatever." Kaylyn tensed. "I'll just finish cooking by myself."

Wordlessly, Mav shifted into the kitchen and began to chop and fry with the aplomb of a chef. Soon, he had brushed Kaylyn from the kitchen altogether in his quest to provide the perfect lunch.

"I'm going to take a shower." Dorian gave Kaylyn a kiss on the cheek and headed off to the bathroom, passing Malachi on the way by, as the latter returned from his girlfriend's prison of fury.

"Hey guys," Malachi said, the apologetic look still in its permanent place. "Sorry about that whole thing."

"Don't worry about it," Travis inserted, Alyssa elbowing him in the ribs for speaking out of turn.

Malachi lowered his voice. "Look, Irina's been a bit…on edge, the past day. She's been trying to call her family back in Russia, but there's no connection and the Wi-Fi is spotty, data isn't working. She hasn't been able to get a call in, and, don't tell her I told you this, but her grandmother is sick and her brother's trying to control the estate. Then there's the fact that she doesn't really know you guys all that well and, she's just upset. Don't take it personally."

"It's all good, we get it," Kaylyn offered with a kind but empty smile.

Malachi glanced to Mav, who avoided looking over. Uncomfortable silence overtook the room, as phones came out of pockets for an extended escape.

"Power's out," Dorian announced, returning to the room with a shrug, half-an-hour later, still towelling off his hair after a very long shower.

Mav whipped around to check his burners and, sure enough, found them cold. "Seriously?"

"How close is it to being done?" Kaylyn inquired, not sure she wanted to know the answer.

"Not very. I'm going to guess it's been out for a while." Mav fished a still-intact block of cheese out of a pot of milk.

"Guess it's chips for breakfast, then." Kaylyn collapsed down onto her elbows, holding her head in frustration while trying to maintain composure.

"Or drive ten miles into town for food," Dorian added.

"Screw it." Kaylyn shook her head and rose back up. "I'm drinking." Pulling glasses from the dishwasher, she began pouring out mimosas for everyone, swigging one back and refilling it before handing the others out to the group.

Headaches miraculously forgotten, they each accepted their offered fare and raised them high. Everyone except Malachi, who, in his embarrassment, had detached himself from the group.

And while the rest were making the best of their misfortune, he decided to hide out outside until the fire of that morning had passed.

No one looked around to notice him opening the patio door. His downcast eyes forgot the warning sign.

The world was copacetic until a loud crack was followed by an alarmed scream.

And they all turned in unison to find Malachi, one leg through the rotted patio wood, the other bent at an awkward angle as he clambered to stay inside, his nails scratching desperately at the linoleum flooring by the door.

He was slipping, fast.

11. Rotten

TRAVIS WAS THE first from his seat, leaping toward the door as his barstool crashed to the ground behind him. He vaulted over two of the couches and fell to the floor as his sock slipped out from under him upon landing. Barely registering the pain, he reached out for Malachi's hand, which, by then, was clawing at the door saddle as the rest of his body curled away into the unknown drop, below.

"I got you, I got you," he soothed futilely, as his hands wrapped around the thick wrist and he was yanked forward by sheer weight. One hand slipped away and the other couldn't hold him.

Travis jammed his foot into the wall and reached down, once again. But the three-hundred-pound man was too much for him, and he could feel his shoulders dislocating, slowly.

Gavin was next into the fray, sliding under Travis' leg and holding out a hand, though he knew he would be able to get no force from his angle. At the least, he could stabilize Malachi. Or, maybe that was wishful thinking.

"Get outta the way," Travis grunted, as his foot came down hard, nearly striking Gavin in the head.

"You need help."

"Yeah, but you're…not…helping!"

Gavin crowded around Travis' other side, searching for a way in, but all angles seemed to be blocked off. Finally, he grabbed Travis around the waist and started pulling. But all that did was start to slide Mala-chi's wrist out from Travis' grip.

"I'm gonna die! I'm gonna die!" Malachi began hyperventilating.

"Not if you shut up and help! Grab the door-frame."

"I can't reach."

Travis angled his pull and tried to drag Malachi closer to the door's edge, with little success.

"Try this." Mav rounded a couch and whipped off his shirt, his baby-fat belly jiggling slightly as he ran. Ducking under Travis, he reached out for Mala-chi's wrist and expertly tied the fabric around it. "I've got a good grip."

"Okay," Travis called. "On three, we pull him to-ward the doorframe and, Malachi, you grab it so we can get an angle under your armpits. One, two, three!"

They pulled, Gavin and Travis tripping over each other, Mav feeling the shirt stretch and start to tear under the immense weight it carried. Malachi's fingers fluttered through the air, trying to find a grip, but he kept falling back, farther and farther.

"One more time," Travis called out, and Mav de-cided against telling the rest that his shirt had, at best, just one more time left in it.

"And if that doesn't work…" Malachi began but could not finish.

"How far is the drop?" Gavin asked.

"It's far. It looks really far—" Malachi peeked down below where, through the darkness, he could spot jagged edges and vicious ground.

"Then we make sure this works." Travis stretched out his neck and tightened his grip.

On three, they pulled, Malachi swinging farther this time, but still he came up just short. The shirt began to tear and Mav leapt forward to grab Malachi's hand, landing half atop the rotted wood and hearing it start to crack beneath him.

Alyssa bolted forward to grab Mav's legs, but found herself thrown forward as Malachi pendulumed back the other way. "Pull!" Mav commanded and she did, as well as she could. "A little more!"

"I'm doing the best I can!"

"Just a few more inches. A few…more…" Malachi gripped the doorframe, which creaked beneath his weight but did not break. Mav let go and allowed Alyssa to pull him back to safety.

"I'm going to get under his left arm; Mav, you get under his right," Travis instructed. "Alyssa, hold me up and Gavin hold Mav." They got into their positions and held tightly.

"Okay, three, two…" Malachi lurched downward. He kicked his legs out uselessly, doing more to shake the foundation of the formation than to assist. He slipped. "GO!"

They pulled as hard as their arms could muster, Malachi slowly but surely rising up above the broken wood.

"A little further!" Travis encouraged, digging his heels into the ground as hard as he could and trying to get enough leverage to extract Malachi from the wood. Malachi lurched back once again. "Be more helpful!"

"I'm trying. I'm trying, but…"

Another yank and his knee was nearly free. Focusing on the ground before him, Malachi tried to swing his leg up, but found it stuck. He tried again, and again, but nothing improved. Finally, with a violent kick downward, he liberated himself enough to drag a thick, heavy leg up over the wooden floor, and he placed as much pressure on it as he could.

They pulled and wrenched and Malachi did all that he could until he was finally free of the hole and lying, face first, on the floor of the house. Travis flew back and fell atop Alyssa, while Gavin and Mav fell off in separate directions, Gavin's head striking the edge of the couch so hard that he was surprised that it drew no blood.

After a few moments of recovery, Malachi started to push himself back up. "I'm so sorry, guys. I wasn't paying attention and forgot about the porch." No one said a word. He threw a hand down in frustration. "I don't mean to keep messing up your weekend."

"No, it's not that. Don't worry about that," Kaylyn instructed.

Malachi accepted the kindness, but felt no less concerned. Looking down at his bloody pantleg, he lifted the torn jeans to discover a long, bleeding gash, accompanied by an unpleasant, oozing white substance that released a powerful odour of death.

The others, collectively, stepped backward in repulsion. "I'd better go shower that off."

"And maybe throw some peroxide on that thing," Travis added.

"Lunch will be ready by the time you're done."
Kaylyn looked to Dorian. "We'll go into town for
subs." Dorian nodded his assent. "Any requests?"

"Keep it simple." Malachi shrugged. "BLT, egg
salad. Whatever, I'll eat it." He patted his stomach.
"Oh," he remembered suddenly, "but Irina's going to
need whole grain bread—not whole wheat, not multi-
grain—she only likes whole grain. And if she has lettuce on hers, she also needs to have hot sauce. But if
there's no lettuce, then kill the hot sauce and replace
it with mayo. Unless there's bacon, in which case the
hot sauce is back on but she also needs to have ham
or pork or some other type of pig-based meat. But
that's not true the other way around, if that makes
sense?"

"Perfectly," Kaylyn lied, resolving to get Irina the
cheapest menu item, regardless of contents.

"Great!" Malachi smiled, though still with a
sheepish bent. "I'm really sorry again, you guys.
Thanks so much for helping me out."

A scattered murmur of 'don't mention it's and
'whatever's spread around the room as he turned for
the bathroom.

Just before entering, however, Malachi paused at
the door, one hand on the frame, and considered for
a second.

"You know," he started with a wry smile, "it's
funny. I know everyone was only trying to pull me
back up. But the weird thing is: the whole time, it felt
like something was pulling me back down." He
chuckled under his breath as Gavin's heart skipped a
beat and Alyssa went cold. "Anyway, see you guys in a

few," he entered the bathroom as though nothing was amiss.

But the thought that he left in his wake was much, much more harrowing than his fall.

12. Discovery

TRAVIS INHALED SLOWLY, letting the rum in his rum and coke burn his nostrils. The laceration on his forehead throbbed as he blinked slowly, eyes fixed upon Gavin on the opposite side of the room. He'd been behaving strangely all day but didn't seem interested in talking about it—which didn't seem like him. For as long as they'd been friends—five years, now, since they'd started, together, at The Palace—Gavin had never been one to keep his emotions to himself. In fact, it got a bit annoying at times.

Something had to be very wrong.

And that led to alcohol.

Travis had watched Gavin drink for a long time, taken in his patterns, come to expect certain tendencies. And, while a tipsy Gavin was a good time, finally able to lay aside the half-baked stressors in favour of peace and pleasure, a drunk Gavin was a liability. He'd spoken out of turn once too often last night, and he would do so again.

And he'd apologize, when he realized what he'd done. He'd apologize for weeks, months, years, even—he still, occasionally, brought up his regret over telling Travis he'd hated his shorter haircut whilst sloshed, four years ago. But the damage would be done.

He could have said anything.

But, he could head him off, Travis thought, if he could just figure out what the hell was messing with him.

And for that matter, what the hell was messing with Alyssa? She'd been strangely chatty all day, for someone whose words, generally, came at a premium. It had taken Travis six months to get more than a few sentences out of her, and another six to coax her into a full conversation. A year after that to get her to go out with him, another three months to get her into bed, and six beyond that before she'd call them official.

But from the other side of the table, this afternoon, she had no interest in shutting up.

"I've never been a big fan of sports, but sometimes we watch them and I start getting into it and I think maybe, but not soccer. Too boring. All they do is run around and nothing ever happens. Maybe basketball. Basketball is more fun…" She hiccoughed and washed it down with what appeared to be a gin and tonic, hold the tonic. Alyssa leaned back in her barstool a little too far and nearly tipped before righting herself.

Under the counter, Travis put a steadying hand on her knee and she gently placed her fingertips on top of his, briefly assuaging his concerns with the tender warmth of love. Because he loved her, and he loved her hard.

"You okay?" he whispered, so no one would hear the tenderness in his voice but for her, so no one would know that he was capable of actually caring.

"Mm." She swallowed and nodded unconvinc-
ingly.

"What's going on?"

She looked away and considered. A moment later,
the front door crashed open, turning all heads away
from the kitchen, and all ears, including Travis', away
from Alyssa's barely whispered response: "I don't like
it here."

Dorian entered with a flourish, two bags of subs
held jubilantly above his head. "Lunch is served."

The group swarmed around, some for energy,
others to sop up the alcohol still dancing about in
their digestive tracts from the night before. Even Irina made her way upstairs at the sound of food.

"This is so good." Brady took a large bite of the
first sandwich he could get his hands on, not waiting
for anyone else to be ready.

Wrappers muffled most other thoughts and
sounds, drowning out Mav's grumble of, "I could've
made better."

Malachi chewed loudly, tongue snapping with
each bite, and it would have been distracting if it
hadn't been nearly three in the afternoon, leaving all
of them famished.

"How was the drive into town?" Alyssa asked
Dorian, seeking comfort in the thought of other people, living people, nearby.

"Basically a ghost town," Dorian managed
through a mouthful of bread, and she winced at that
word. "Felt like we were the only ones there…and the
sub guy, of course."

"Great…" Alyssa slunk back in her chair and downed the rest of her drink.

"There is not enough chipotle mayonnaise on my sub," Irina complained sharply, and the absent sub guy had everything to fear despite her distance. "And it is not toasted. How you eat these untoasted, I will not understand." In a huff, she stormed across the kitchen and tried to turn on the stove. No one bothered to tell her that the power was out.

"Wait," Kaylyn commanded, counting heads just as Mallory peeked out from the staircase, still in pyjamas, sleep in her eyes. "Ten. Who's missing?"

"Is Mick still asleep?" Gavin glanced to the stairs.

"Don't wake him up," Brady warned. "He'll be pissy all day."

"Well, if he wants to waste the weekend he's paying for, fine. That's his problem," Kaylyn said coldly. "What about Torri and Jim? Are they still outside working out?"

General shrugs waved around the room, no one especially noticing or caring, nor wanting to engage Kaylyn's wrath.

"Are you kidding me?" she cried. "Can't even be bothered to hang out with the rest of us for *one* weekend? Seriously?"

"I wouldn't worry too much about it," Alyssa offered. "They probably just want to finish up and then they'll feel better hanging out and doing nothing for the rest of the day."

"They work out every day for hours," Kaylyn snapped. "One day won't kill them."

Alyssa raised her hands defensively and backed away into her seat. *Okay, you do you, sis*, she thought, averting eye contact.

"Irina, can you go get my brother, *please?*"

"Why me?" Irina's falcon eyes turned on her menacingly. "Trying to get me out of the room so I am not spoiling your little party?"

Most of the room curled in the opposite direction, assuming the air raid position, but Kaylyn was too miffed to be intimidated. "*Or*, because you're the only one standing close to the door."

"I cannot do it." She turned back to her still-cold sub. "Do it yourself."

Gavin bit his lip as Kaylyn balled her fists and, though she was pencil-thin and had probably never had a biceps muscle in her life, that did not appear to matter to her as she prepared her attack.

"You know, when you're invited somewhere…" Kaylyn began.

"You want to finish that sentence?" Irina turned, hand closing on a kitchen knife she'd been using to pare the edges off her sandwich, with army precision.

"…the least you could do…"

"I'll go!" Gavin volunteered a little too aggressively, in hopes of restoring equilibrium. And for a chance to get out of the house, if just for a moment.

Though Kaylyn went silent, she and Irina continued their violent staring contest, each daring the other to move.

As Gavin pressed through the front door, he realized, suddenly, just how dark it had gotten since he'd woken up a few hours previous. Gone was the clean sixty-degree sun, and a frigid chill had entered the air under the ashy clouds. A crash of thunder greeted his first footstep onto the dirt driveway that extended around the side of the house and into the weeds of the backyard.

He hugged his thin, button-up shirt around himself, suddenly wishing he'd thrown on a sweater for the thirty second walk. He equally hugged the side of the house, not knowing what kind of animal might lurk in the dense forest to this left. A duck quacked. He jumped. He rolled his eyes. He continued.

Torri and Jim were not next to the back porch. Gavin peered over the drop-off that led down to the firepit and flatter ground below. "Hey!" he called. "Torri? Jim? Lunch is ready."

They did not respond from where they were positioned, a few feet back of the pit's jagged rocks.

Gavin hesitated at the edge of the stony steps. Now, in the daylight, it was clear just how steep they were, and it seemed a miracle that any of them had made it down safely in the dark. Vertigo set in and he stepped back, but a glance at the house reminded him of the war that was brewing, and it seemed the only choice was forward.

Leaning backward, Gavin eased his way from thin, unstable stone to thinner, more unstable stone, breath held and eyes away from the ground. The first raindrop hit him in the forehead. The second, in the right eye.

"Torri? Jim?" he tried again—halfway down, now. But like everything else, he supposed, his voice must have been eaten up in the dead silence of the place.

Toeing around hesitantly, Gavin found that he'd reached the bottom. With a sigh of relief, he levelled his gaze and turned to face Torri and Jim, spread out on their exercise mats in the middle of the yard.

Not feeling the rain. Not feeling the cold.

Not feeling anything at all.

Because, the moment Gavin laid eyes on the blood strewn across the dewy weeds, he knew that they were dead.

13. Panic

THE JAGGED STONE that teetered on the edge of the firepit was slimed with brain matter. Jim's left eye had been gouged out of its socket. Torri's mouth gaped widely in a scream, almost as large as the gape in his throat. Legs were strewn in all the wrong directions, an arm was smashed and turned around at the elbow.

And the rain began to wash it all away.

Gavin didn't know how long he stood there, staring at the horror. He didn't know how long he'd been screaming or why his throat hurt as much as it did. But his feet wouldn't move and his brain would not process. The rain soaked the clothes to his skin, but his heart had started to beat blood so cold that he barely noticed the icy temperatures beating down upon him.

It was Travis' voice that woke him, cutting through the violent, guttural cry that permeated the air, which Gavin realized must have been his own. "What's going on? Gavin! What the hell…?"

Travis stopped dead, mid-sentence, one hand slowly slipping off Gavin's shoulder as he turned the corner at the bottom of the rocky, now slippery, stairs and took in the fates of Torri and Jim.

"But…how…?" was all Travis could manage, and it was more than Gavin was capable of.

Brain rushing quickly, Travis ran to the stairs, where most of the rest of the group was making its way down to find out what all the ruckus was about. "Stay up there," Travis commanded. "No one come down."

But it was too late for Kaylyn, already staring upon the mess that was her brother's corpse from the third step up. "No!" she cried out, racing forward instinctively. Her flats slipped on the slick stone and sent her flying through the air, but she barely noticed as Travis caught her mid-fall and held her around the waist in a death grip, allowing none to pass, no matter how hard she pulled against him, crying out in agonized wails.

There was no stopping them, now, as others crowded around. Alyssa lost her breath and instinctively sat on the bottom step. Mallory vomited into the weeds. Dorian, composed and breathing slowly, walked sombrely to the front and took Kaylyn from Travis, his touch more easily directing her away from the carnage, despite her protests.

"I knew there were bears out here," Brady pronounced, checking over his shoulder and squinting into the forest. "Guys, we gotta get outta here. There's bears!"

But as Mav and Malachi began a slow backward step away, Irina, unfazed, pushed her way past Mallory and Alyssa, knocked Kaylyn with her shoulder, and approached the sordid scene contemplatively.

"No, not bears," she proclaimed after a few moments' inspection.

"Get away from him! Get away from them!" Kaylyn cried as Dorian wrapped her in a tight hug and held her back from charging the tall, wispy Russian.

Irina didn't even look back at the hysterical woman behind her. "You see"—she crouched down and, without making contact, drew a line across Jim's neck—"this one. He was strangled first. Then bludgeoned with the rock." She gestured casually toward the jagged stone, brain matter slowly dripping down into the grass. "And this one…" She approached Torri, stroking her chin in consideration. "This is stab wound." She pointed to a hole beneath Torri's torso. "Again, the rock—you can see the brain of that one on his shirt. Then neck sliced, of course."

"H-how do you know that…?" Alyssa managed, half-amazed, half-suspicious.

From the back of the group, Malachi piped up weakly: "She was a doctoral student, in Russia, before she came here."

Alyssa opened her mouth in comprehension, feeling the urge to apologize for never having gotten to know Irina despite working with her for five years. But, she didn't have to think hard to realize that the time and place were wrong, and the odour of blood wafting across her tongue was enough to shut her mouth.

"This is no bear," Irina repeated, now looking up at the group, coldly, matter-of-factly. "This is murder."

"No!" Kaylyn called out, bursting forward, but only half out of Dorian's grasp, as he dragged her back around the stomach. "Who did this? Who the hell…? No, this doesn't make any sense. It's lies!

Lies!" She jabbed a finger aggressively at Irina, but as she screamed and cursed at the stoic Russian, her voice began to fade.

"Okay," Dorian soothed her, "okay, we're going to figure this out. We're going to figure something out. We'll get to the bottom of this…"

"I'm gonna kill someone; I'm gonna kill whoever did this!" Kaylyn cried out, but it was now more of a whimper.

Still clutching her around the middle, Dorian turned back to the rest of the group. "Someone, call 9-1-1. Tell them to get out here as fast as they can."

Silence. Mav lurched for his phone but immediately stopped himself. Gavin checked just to be sure, his shaking hand struggling to force its way in and out of his pocket.

Quietly, dry mouth sticking to itself and throat burning from the screaming, he said, "No bars."

"No bars," Malachi confirmed.

"Right." Dorian took a breath. "Can someone call over Wi-Fi?"

"Wi-Fi's out," Brady reminded him.

And before Dorian could suggest it, Alyssa meekly noted, "No data out here, either."

"Any chance there was a landline?" But no one even bothered to justify that with a response.

After a moment of tense, sickening quiet, Travis spoke up: "Look, even if we could call, it's not safe for us all to stick around here if there's a murderer on the loose. We have to get back into town. Now."

"There are only three cars," Gavin managed.

"And Jim was one of the drivers," Alyssa finished.

"It's fine; I'll drive Jim's car." Travis took charge, though he shook as he said it.

"You're concussed," Alyssa reminded him.

"I'm not concussed!" he snapped before shaking his head and mouthing 'sorry' in her direction. He re-started more calmly, "I'm not concussed. It's just some mild headaches. And now is not the time to think about safe driving. We have to get away from here."

"All right," Dorian agreed. "We'll figure out driving arrangements once we're back in the city. For now, we get out of here as fast as we can. Someone go and get Jim's keys."

"I'll get Mick!" Brady offered, rushing off.

"Wait!" Travis called after him. But he was gone before anyone could offer to accompany him for safety.

"There is nothing here." Irina wiped her hands against her pyjama pants after tapping the pocketless sides of both Jim and Torri's pants. "Someone must check the room."

"I'll do it," Kaylyn volunteered weakly, as the rain matted her long black hair across her face wildly.

"No," Travis insisted, blocking her path as she pulled—somewhat in control of herself, now—away from Dorian, and stumbled toward the stairs. "You should sit down."

"He's my brother!" she shot back. "No one's touching his stuff, but me."

"I don't know if that's…" Travis began, pressing through despite the unrelenting aggression in Kaylyn's eyes.

"It's fine, I'll go with her," Mallory offered through a gulp of swallowed sick.

"I will, too." Gavin led the way, even the house seeming more comforting than this scene.

"Okay." Travis nodded once. "We reconvene in the kitchen. Get anything you absolutely, one-hundred-percent need, and nothing else. We leave in ten minutes."

14. Hunting

"MICK! MICK!" BRADY'S cry rang out through the house as he rushed down the stairs, tripping on the way and landing in a heap at the bottom before slowly stretching his way back up and racing for their shared bedroom.

Behind him, Gavin practically dragged Kaylyn and Mallory through the door to Jim and Torri's room yelling, "Where would they be? Where would they be?"

"I don't know!" Kaylyn retorted frustratedly.

She made for a pile of clothes at the end of the bed and threw shirts and yoga pants aside, finding nothing with a logical pocket. "The fanny pack, pass me the fanny pack." She reached out demandingly and Mallory grabbed the small, black pleather case, which Kaylyn promptly yanked from her hands.

Nothing. "Look for bags," Kaylyn commanded, "or their suitcases. Or anything." She threw open two drawers to no avail. "But don't open them. Pass them to me. Only I open things."

Mallory checked under the bed, on nightstands. Gavin sifted through a pile of clothes that may or may not have already been checked.

*

BRADY BURST INTO the bedroom, limping, his ankle having been caught under his back in the fall.

"Mick!" he screamed, out of breath. "Get up! Come on, man!"

Mick did not stir.

Brady stepped toward Mick's bed, cocking his head to verify that the lump under the sheets was, indeed, Mick. "Mick. We gotta go! Someone killed those two dudes. Mick!"

The bed remained still.

*

"FOUND THEM!" MALLORY called out, reaching under Jim's bed for a crumpled mass underneath. She came out with a large spider in her palm. She screamed. "Get it off me!"

Gavin leapt up, smacking his head on a side table. "What is that?"

Mallory shook her hand wildly, sending the spider careening through the air as Gavin jumped back, barely evading contact with the creeping, black thing, but jamming his tailbone hard into the room's doorhandle. "Argh!"

Kaylyn kept on searching, as though nothing had happened, now throwing objects wildly from the 'unchecked' side of the room to the 'checked' side. "They're not here! They're not *here!*"

*

"MAN, WAKE UP. Please." Brady had stopped screaming and his heart had started racing. If Mick wasn't there, in that bed, that could only mean…

No, he wouldn't believe that Mick was the killer. He couldn't have been. Always a legalist, one of the good ones. Breathing heavily, heart pumping now more from fear than from his run, Brady reached a hand out toward the amorphous blob of sheets.

*

KAYLYN STRUCK A wall with her bare, open hand, barely leaving a mark and not yet feeling the pain that would come later. "Pass me Jim's pants, again."

Gavin winced as he bent and grabbed the jeans, patting them down before tossing them over.

Kaylyn tried, desperately, to dig her hands into the tight pockets. "Where could they be?" She faded from upset to lost. "They *have to* be here."

"Pass me the clothes," Mallory instructed. "One by one." She stomped at the spider, but it scurried under the dresser.

Gavin, rushing to the opposite side of the room, began throwing her garments, which Mallory shook out and deposited on the bed. A small baggie of powder dropped from one of the pockets and Mallory surreptitiously booted it under the bed, lest Kaylyn see.

Kaylyn checked the sheets once more, the suitcases. "I know he brought them inside with him," Kaylyn moaned. "I remember him talking about putting them away at one point. He said something. They have to be in here."

"They're not," Mallory finally concluded, shaking out the last sweater. "They're not here."

*

BRADY'S FINGERTIPS GRAZED the comforter and felt nothing. Just the soft give of fabric. He glanced back over his shoulder, quickly, half-expecting to see Mick standing there, clad in black, weapon brandished. But no one. Just loud, fat spatters of rain against the window. A fork of lightning cut across the room.

Brady returned to Mick's bed and, with an empty breath, shot both hands forward and grabbed the sheets. "Last chance, Micky," he whispered as a boom of thunder underscored his rapid heartbeat. He tore the sheets away.

Something fell away from beneath the covers and rolled straight for Brady. With a yelp, he jumped back, stumbling over his ankles and pitching to the ground. The thing rolled to a stop at the tip of his toe. And Mick's severed head looked up at Brady, eyes blank and hollow. Another flash of lightning, and Brady's vision blurred in madness.

*

TRAVIS HELD HIS hand out for the keys the moment Kaylyn, Mallory, and Gavin returned from Jim and Torri's room. "Let's go."

Heads hung low, Gavin avoided eye contact; Mallory proceeded in a dazed stupor; and Kaylyn,

98

fighting back the tears threatening to cut through her cheeks, passed on the news that none of them could bear to hear: "They're not there."

Travis looked slightly stupefied. "But, they have to be somewhere."

"They have to be there," Kaylyn agreed. "They have to, but they're not. I don't know where they are. I looked everywhere. I looked *everywhere*, I swear." She started to cry and Dorian swiftly moved to hold her.

"I know. We all know. There's nothing more you could've done," he soothed.

"There has to be something." She tried to push him away, but he was strong despite his medium figure—or, she was weak or, perhaps, both.

"Now what?" Alyssa squeaked.

"DEAD!"

The cry came from down the stairs, and they turned to face the source of the voice.

Brady raced up the stairs, eyes hollow and brain overloaded. "He's dead! He's dead. Mick's dead. Ohmygodohmygodohmygod. He's DEAD!"

"Brady, what happened?" Dorian took a step forward, directing the rest to stay back as he stood as if prepared to block the much larger and hysterical man.

"Someone chopped off his head! There's…"— he choked from running too hard— "so…much…*blood!*"

He reached the top of the stairs, his face contorted in fear, disgust, and hopelessness. "I didn't know what to do. I just…I sat there and didn't…I ran upstairs…and…"

As Brady stepped forward, his leg caught in a low-lying rope that was strung across the living room floor.

He had just enough time to look down and see what had ensnared him before the rope yanked taut like a shot. Though a bigger man, he was no match for the unexpected force of the rope, which dragged him to the ground, smashing his head before raising him in the air, where it was tied off against one of the high wooden rafters in the ceiling.

Alyssa screamed. Malachi grabbed his heart.

And for a moment, Brady hung before them, suspended upside down by a single ankle, flailing wildly.

"Keep still!" Travis called out, eyes widening with shock. But Brady could not keep still. He sputtered and spasmed and tried to wrench himself free of the simple, yet terrifying, trap. "You're putting too much pressure on…" Travis rushed forward, eyes to the ceiling. But he was too late.

The rafter creaked and the crack echoed throughout the room as it split in two and sent Brady, head-first, into the ground.

He landed with a thwack and a stream of blood that slowly started trickling onto the floor. His eyes were open, but there was nothing behind them. Because his neck was turned nearly halfway around. Broken. Horrid. Dead.

15. Chaos

THE INSTINCTIVE PUSH backward cycled into the uncertain desire to reach the front door. But Brady lay in the way.

Travis broke the single moment of stasis by rushing forward to check on the fallen sommelier and, from there, chaos erupted.

Gavin and Malachi broke for the sliding back doors, only to remember the sign advertising the inevitable fall through the patio. Alyssa and Mallory collided, and though the slight and wispish Alyssa managed to hold her balance whilst stumbling backward, Mallory had never possessed strong stability and spun her way to the floor. Irina knocked into Kaylyn on the way to the door and, though it was likely unintentional, Kaylyn shoved back, sending Irina careening to the ground, just feet away from Brady's body.

Malachi spun around and raced wildly for the opposite side of the room, his shin connecting hard with the back of Mallory's head as she attempted to get up. Her forehead slammed into the ground and she felt the spin of dizziness wash over her. Dorian was the next to experience Malachi's three-hundred-pound blow as, looking the wrong way, the giant of a man ploughed straight into the six-foot blonde, making him seem suddenly childlike in comparison. Dorian flew back and caught himself against the wall, where his outstretched leg caught Alyssa's ankle and sent her into Malachi's back.

Mav, swerving to avoid a wildly panicked Gavin on one side and Kaylyn, retreating from Irina's death search, on the other, bent down to try to help Mallory back up, only to have Irina clip his back heel on the way by, sending him down on top of the crumpled girl.

Travis leaned in close to Brady's broken frame. He was still, no breath in his chest, but something fluttered in his face. As he neared, Brady's lips moved, just slightly. "What was that?" Travis pressed his ear as close as he dared to the crumpled figure, blood stinging his nose. But Brady said nothing, his body still moving in death, but his brain gone. Just as Travis was set to move away, the rope gave its final lurch, sending Brady's heavy leg down, across Travis' face, and knocking his cheek into the pool of blood that rippled around Brady's split head.

Dorian slunk to the floor against the wall and crawled over to where Alyssa was sprawled out, near the door to the garage. He grabbed her arm and helped to hoist her back up as he did the same with himself. "Stay calm," he commanded, but Alyssa couldn't hear him over the whir of her own brain.

As she turned to rush away, Alyssa screamed, pointing in terror at Travis in the centre of the room, his face caked in red as he backed slowly from Brady's corpse. "Travis!" she recovered enough to croak out before running to him.

"I'm fine! I'm fine," he yelled over the screams. "It's not mine." But she'd wrapped her arms around him and, not knowing what else to do, he held her back, gently, eyes still fixed on Brady, blinking away the dripping blood.

"Everyone, stop!" Dorian called out, but no one could hear him.

Malachi burst through the garage door to find the room filled with storage equipment: kerosene lamps, tools, a rusty old engine. But no egress.

Irina caught up with Kaylyn and slew footed her to the floor. Kaylyn slid along the hardwood and hopped back up in a fluid motion, ready to charge at her pursuer, but not ready quickly enough. Irina was already on top of her, long and sharpened false fingernails clutching at both of Kaylyn's arms. "Hey!" Kaylyn screamed as the nails dug in, stomping wildly in search of Irina's foot as she was ostensibly carried into the wall.

"Calm down!" Dorian cried.

Gavin yanked violently at the window in Kaylyn and Dorian's room, not caring about the fall to the ground twenty feet below or the violent rain that had darkened the world so profusely that nothing was visible beyond the panes. It was unlocked and flew open so fast that he hit himself in the face with his own surprised fist. He shook his head, regained composure. But the moment he looked outside, a violent streak of lightning forked across the sky, blinding him, threatening to take him if he dared step out into the storm, while the mud below flowed, a thrashing river of quicksand.

Mav lifted Mallory to her feet and she stumbled forward. He grabbed for her, but she fell again, taking him down with her. Mav's head struck the ground and he yelped, feeling for blood and finding his hand covered in sticky red. But a quick glance to his right showed his proximity to Brady and, with half-relief, half-concern, Mav realized that he didn't know whether the blood was his or part of the pool he'd fallen into. No time to consider, he wrenched himself back up and helped Mallory more slowly, this time.

She was just stabilizing as Travis and Alyssa, looking in the opposite direction, neared in their retreat from the centre of the room. Mav charged and wrapped them in a bearhug to block Mallory, but sent all three into an awkward side-step dance in the process.

Malachi tripped on his way up the stairs and out of the garage and slammed his already bloodied leg hard into the top step. He wailed but kept running, circling his arms as he plummeted to the floor.

Frustrated and finished, Dorian whistled loudly, the screech echoing off the high ceilings and piercing the ears of the room. "EVERYONE SETTLE DOWN!"

Mav dug in a heel to stabilize Alyssa and Travis.

Malachi peeled himself into a kneeling position.

Gavin rushed in from the bedroom to survey the commotion.

Mallory took a knee, shutting her eyes tightly.

Kaylyn and Irina froze, mid-tussle, Irina's hands perilously close to Kaylyn's neck, and Kaylyn's foot an inch behind Irina's left ankle.

All eyes turned to Dorian. Aside from Travis' left eye, which still blinked Brady's blood away.

Dorian embraced the silence, letting his footsteps ring out as he took six firm steps into the centre of the living room and hopped up onto the arm of one of the couches. "We *need* to stay calm. I know that's not easy right now, but the only way we're all getting outta here alive is if we take things slowly and logically from here. Anyone disagree?"

Irina looked ready to speak up but, remembering her proximity to Kaylyn's fury, decided not to turn her attention fully from her sparring partner.

"Good." He took a moment to scan the room: plates still piled up on the kitchen island; the lion poster on the wall now sporting a mysterious slash through its centre; the high, pitched ceiling shadowed in darkness—natural light now a thing of memory in the storm.

"Okay," he continued, "the plan hasn't changed, just the logistics. There are"—he did a quick head count—"nine of us left. We don't have Jim and Torri's keys, but we still have two sedans. That's ten seats. We head back into town, tell the police everything, and go from there."

"We need Mick's keys," Travis noted, dragging a sleeve across his bloodied face.

"I'll get them…" Mav offered with a glance around at the other, hesitant faces.

"We go together," Dorian pronounced. "No splitting up, no separation." He hopped down from the leather arm and led the pack to the stairs.

Slipping around Brady—some, like Malachi, Mallory, and Gavin, avoiding the sight—they took the steps slowly. Kaylyn pushed Irina off, moving her foot to avoid tripping the Russian. The fire had passed and productivity took precedence, now. Irina still offered a glare in return, but she followed the group, all the same.

The basement was black, and Dorian flicked his phone light on, swinging it side to side to guide the rest along the way, in a kind of wave that left some feeling as though they were rocking along rough waters in an unseaworthy ship.

"Before we go in here"—Dorian stopped outside of the door to face the group—"remember that Mick's still inside. It may not be pretty, but we have to do this, and we have to do it as a collective. So, no one scream. No one run. Just look at the ceiling if you need to but, whatever you do, *don't panic*."

He turned and led the way through the open door.

The bed was piled high with the sheets, and the body remained blocked from sight by the door. It would have seemed little more than an untidy room if not for Mick's head, still staring blindly up at the ceiling from near the wall, where Brady had inadvertently kicked it in his race to get away.

Heart sinking slightly, Mav compartmentalized his fear for the moment and strode determinedly across the room to Brady's bed, where he wrenched a sheet from the bed and threw it overtop of Mick's head.

"I'll check his bag," Travis offered, dropping to his knees and sifting through bottles of vodka, gin, mojito mix.

Kaylyn started methodically upon the clothes piled in the corner of the room without a word, tossing the empty-pocketed garments to Mallory, who caught and dropped.

"Nothing," they both concluded, almost simultaneously.

Dorian glanced around the room, lips pursed. "Someone…"

"Someone has to check the body," Gavin finished, breathless.

Silence persisted, everyone glancing at those around them while avoiding eyes at the same time.

Irina examined the headless figure. "He has been dead for some time," she mused. "Rigor mortis has set in. He will not move when you touch him." She said this as if it was supposed to be reassuring but she equally didn't seem to care that it had the opposite effect on most.

Finally, Mav stepped forward. "I'll do it."

"You're a saint, Maverick Chow," Malachi murmured, garnering him a sharp look from Irina.

Mav swallowed hard and rolled his shoulders back, trying to mentally prepare.

"Just do it fast," Dorian advised quietly.

Mav nodded once and stepped next to the bed, staring down at the deep red stains and the mangled, stringy top of Mick's neck. He closed his eyes and slid his hands toward the beige sheets, struggling to get under them while making as little contact as possible with the body. He patted around uselessly, not knowing if he'd found shirt, pants or bed. His fingers brushed over the groin and his eyes shot open. He was going to have to look, no choice now.

Mav pulled the sheets aside and Gavin gasped, Mallory dry retched, Malachi shielded his eyes. "I have to turn him," Mav warned after patting down the side pockets to no avail.

No one spoke, though Kaylyn sat down against the doorframe and mouthed, head in hands, "Why is this happening, why is this happening?"

Taking a shoulder and a hip, Mav flipped the corpse as gently as he could. He already had one body's blood on him, there was no point in shying away from a second. Mick was surprisingly heavy in death and, though Mav was not weak, he struggled to lift and flip him. And all was for nought, anyway. It only took a moment to see that Mick didn't have back pockets on his pants.

Mav shook his head. "Nothing."

"That's okay," Dorian soothed.

"HOW IS THAT OKAY?" Gavin snapped, breathing heavily, nearly hyperventilating. "That was our last chance. What're we gonna do? Strap four of us to the roof?" He turned to the room hysterically. "Anyone know how to hotwire a car?"

"Gavin, Gavin." Dorian approached from behind and laid a hand upon Gavin's tense back. "We'll figure it out…"

"I say we run." Gavin shook. "All of us. He, she, it, whatever—they can't get us all."

"No one runs," Dorian commanded, still speaking softly, but clearly in control. "Just sit down, Gavin. Sit over there, on Brady's bed. Come on." He guided Gavin to the bed with some difficulty. "There you go." He eased the other man down and returned to the rest of the room.

"I mean, he's not *wrong*," Travis cut in. "We need to get out of here somehow, and if we can't drive…"

"We just have to change tactics." Dorian raised a hand to arrest other speech. "Clearly, we can't all go, anymore. But that's okay. I have a plan."

"Who made you the boss of us?" Irina stepped forward, ready to usurp leadership, but Malachi, of all people, held her shoulder. And what she took from him in mental power, he had not lost in brute strength. She struggled in his grip but, regret in his eyes, he refused to let go.

"Let the man speak," he managed.

Dorian nodded once in thanks, "We need to stick together as much as we can, but obviously that's not completely possible, now. So, I'm going to drive into town. I'll get police; I'll bring back cars. I'll drive as fast as I can—probably better if I get pulled over, anyway.

"As for the rest of you, just stay here, in the same room. Use the buddy system, whatever. Just don't get split up. We're only safe when we're all together."

"Then you shouldn't go alone." Kaylyn rose, shaking her head. "I'll come with you."

"No, it's safer if you're here with the rest of the group." Dorian seemed restless now, dancing in the direction of the door, like there was no time to waste.

"But *you* won't be safe."

"I'll be in a car and I'll be away from here. I'll be fine. It's the people *here* who need as much buffering as possible, not me."

"That's dumb," Travis contested.

"It's the only way," Dorian snapped, unable to keep still, now.

He pressed through the group and led the way back upstairs, around Brady and into the main hall. "Nobody leaves this house." He walked backward toward the door. "I'll be back as soon as I can." He rested his hand upon the knob and turned, rainwater flying wildly into the house and soaking the front mat. "And remember"—he pulled the keys from his pocket and pointed at each one of them, individually, before disappearing into the stormy black—"no one splits up."

16. Separation

"WE NEED TO split up."

"Honestly, of all the people to have the dumbest idea all day, I thought it would be Irina, not you, Gavin." Travis casually passed Irina, her fists balled, to face Gavin head-on. He took his friend's shoulders and bent down a few inches to look him straight in the eyes. "We're not safe alone. You *know* that."

Gavin pulled away, needing space to breathe. "I know, but we're also not safe as a group, anyway."

Mallory shook her head. "Look, if we all just sit here in the kitchen…"

"This *thing* is going to pick us off one by one," Gavin cut in. "Just like it did with Brady, right in front of us." He looked around the room, defying anyone to argue with him on that point. No one did. "And Mick—he was killed in the house, when we were all here. This thing doesn't care where we are or who we're with. It's coming for us and it's going to get us. Honestly, Dorian's the only safe one, being out of here."

"*This thing, this thing.*" Irina scoffed, glaring him down. "You talk like it is not one of us who is doing this."

"Because it's not." Gavin paused to let the words take effect. "Come on," he prodded, seeing the blank stares, pitying him in the loss of his sanity. "You heard what DJ said when he took us on the tour of the house. Travis, Alyssa, Mav, Irina—you weren't there—but the rest of you. *He said this place was haunted.*"

For a moment, the room hung in uncomfortable silence, before Travis stepped forward and gently prodded Gavin out of the centre of their makeshift circle in the kitchen—the furthest part of the main room from Brady's corpse.

"Gav, I love you," Travis began, "but you're nuts."

"You people tire me." Irina rolled her eyes from the far side of the island. "And you." She indicated Gavin with a dismissive flick of a finger. "You are either fool or murderer, but I will not listen to any more of your tired illogic. I am going to my bedroom." She pushed her way through the kitchen, bumping into people as she passed and ignoring their grunts and 'hey's. Gavin stood stunned as she brushed by him, his stomach churning over the accusation that had been thrown his way.

"Irina! Irina, wait!" Malachi called after her, chasing her down through the kitchen, though it may have been easier to take the other side of the island. He took her wrist but she shimmied it off.

"You"—she pointed a long, black fingernail in his face—"do not tell me what to do."

"We can't be alone down there," Malachi pleaded. "It's not safe."

She had already turned and was heading back toward the stairs, Brady now being used as a separator between them. "You stay if you must. I do not care. Be with your friends. But I go down, and that is the end of the story!"

Malachi flinched as she disappeared from sight, glanced back at the kitchen. And finally, deflated, he returned to the group.

"Doesn't matter," Gavin muttered.

"Hey now." Malachi shot up defensively, but Gavin shook his head.

"Not like that. Unless we get some answers into what this thing is and why it's doing this, it doesn't matter where we are or what we do. It's going to get us."

"Can you stop talking crazy for a sec?" Travis raised his hands in a simmer-down manner.

"Yeah, Gav. There are no ghosts," Mallory concurred. "Stop worrying about that."

"It's okay, man." Mav dropped a hand on Gavin's back and, out of respect, he let it rest there, though he wanted to shake it off.

"Guys, trust me, I wouldn't be saying this unless I *really* believed it. I know it sounds crazy. But it's true. I heard it."

Mav's hand slowly slipped away.

"Heard what?" Travis prodded skeptically.

"I heard the ghost. Last night, coming from behind that locked door downstairs. It was screaming." He was met with skeptical glances.

"It's true," Alyssa piped up meekly. All heads shot in her direction and she took an instinctive step back. Swallowing, she continued. "I—I heard it, too. Gavin and I—we tried to open the door but it was impossible, and then it stopped. But we both heard the same thing. It was a person, screaming."

A blast of thunder punctuated the silence that the rest of the room fell under.

Malachi glanced back at the stairs, wondering if he should pursue his girlfriend. Travis slowly edged his way around the island to where Alyssa stood, opposite him. "Is there any chance," he started, running a hand through his long, bloody hair, "is there any chance, it was the boiler?"

Alyssa looked him dead in the eyes, her deep, cerulean irises piercing through him, inviting him into her mind. And firmly, in a level tone, she pronounced, "It was not the boiler."

Travis sucked his lip in. "Mick? Could it have been Mick?"

"It was a woman."

Travis curled his hands, trying to dry the sweat away against more sweat. "Okay," he began, hesitatingly, "let's say for a second that, maybe, there's an outside chance, that there's a ghost in here."

"There is," Alyssa and Gavin corrected, in unison.

"Maybe," Travis insisted, once more. "But what can we do about it, then? Aside from going outside. And, honestly, if this *isn't* a ghost, I'd rather us all be in here, together, than outside, in the dark, where we can't see a damn thing in the middle of a freakin' forest."

"We have to find out what the story is," Gavin determined.

"He didn't tell you?"

"The others sent him away before he could." Gavin tried to say it as unaccusatorially as possible, but he caught Kaylyn and Mallory looking to the floor, out the corner of his eye.

"Well, it's a little late now…" Travis grimaced.

"Not necessarily." Gavin looked around the room, seeking out every eye that evaded his gaze. "DJ told us where he lives. First house down the street, about two miles away. Can't miss it, only other house on the street, he said."

Travis looked to the front window and scoffed at the near pitch blackness, although it was only 4:30 in the afternoon. "You wanna take a forty-five-minute hike out in *that?*"

"It's the only way." And to punctuate his point, a crash of thunder shook the house so severely that a glass fell from the counter and shattered on the floor by Alyssa's feet. She leapt back, unscathed, as Mav set about picking up the pieces.

Travis mulled this over as the rest of the room watched in anticipation; anxiety. When he spoke again, the disbelief and doubt in his tone had been replaced with more pliable uncertainty. He toed at the floor in contemplation. "I just don't see how it, practically, works…I mean, we all just go traipsing down the street in the middle of a storm?"

"I'm not going out there in this weather," Malachi stated, but voice more quavering with fear than demanding with the bravado of his girlfriend.

"No, we shouldn't all go," Gavin agreed.

"Then who?"

"I'll go," Gavin volunteered immediately. "Better than sitting around here and waiting to die."

"Well, if you put it that way, I guess I'll go with you," Kaylyn said, partially wanting to get away from Irina, partially wanting a distraction so she wouldn't have to think about Dorian's absence, partially preferring to spend time in the company of someone she trusted rather than the group that had continually let her down over the weekend.

"Then I'm in," Mallory rushed to offer, ready to support Kaylyn in anything, even if she immediately regretted her decision.

They looked around for more takers. Mav bit his lip. "I could probably go, too…"

"I think it's enough at three," Travis cut in quickly, glancing over at Mav. "We don't want to deplete the group at the house too much, in case it's *not* a supernatural entity doing this."

"What if there's an attack in the woods?" Mav pointed out.

"We don't have any reason to believe there are killers out there, aside from animals. At least, not anymore. In here, it's a hell of a lot more likely."

"What if a bear attacks them?" Alyssa twirled a finger in Travis' shirt nervously.

"Honestly, at that point, I don't think having more people's gonna help much."

"I don't know…" Mav hummed, still feeling a pull to go with his friends.

"No," Travis said with finality. "There's no point in it. We might as well keep as many of us together as we can."

"Three is enough," Gavin agreed. And, though he would have liked to have more company, he understood the argument. "It's raining like crazy out there, anyway. No point in everyone being uncomfortable and heavy for the rest of the night when we're trying to run away from ghosts."

Kaylyn nodded. "Then we should go, soon. Get this over with."

Gavin was already walking toward the front door. "Let's go."

17. Nightwalk

THE ROAD TO Hell was unpaved.

The sole streetlight out front of The Little Maple Cabin was blurred in the whipping rain until it could have passed for a jaundiced moon, had there been one that night. Instead, it provided a very fleeting signpost to follow in the general direction of the street. Beyond that, it was a distant memory, sucked into the vacuum of invisible space.

Mallory glanced back, squinted, tried to see the house, but it was gone to the devil, within a few short steps past humanity.

Her heart dropped into her stomach and a chill ran through her. A chill that almost warmed her up in the frigid night air.

Not night, she reminded herself—they all, simultaneously, reminded themselves. It wasn't even five in the afternoon. If not for the storm, the sun would still be setting on an otherwise warm November day.

"I wanna go back!" Mallory yelled over the pound of the storm, but thunder swallowed out her cry, sending her three feet into the air, and she didn't dare repeat the words she longed to say. She wasn't cut out for this kind of thing. She was an indoorsy type, who enjoyed coffee and television by the fire. Or, in lieu of a fire, a nice, heated blanket. Peace, simplicity, and a good pension. Being out, in the middle of nowhere, was fine enough on the inside, pushing the limits by the fire pit, and well out of bounds in the fires of Hell.

"How much farther?" she cried out, this time uninterrupted by nature.

"We just left," Gavin called back.

Had they really? It felt like forever. Even Gavin was questioning his timelines, though he felt fairly certain they *must* have just left.

The ghost was messing with his head. That was what he concluded.

They walked in silence for a while, trying to focus on anything but the world around them. But the steps didn't seem to take them anywhere, and nothing about the trek felt right.

"Are we still on the path?" Kaylyn finally inquired.

"Y—" Gavin began, but stomping his foot down, he could no longer tell if he felt grass, dirt, or just the lake in his shoe. "I think so," he concluded, in a low tone of contemplation.

Ahead, a bolt of fork lightning sliced through the sky, illuminating the silhouettes of giant trees and empty roads. They *were* on the path, and they breathed a collective sigh of relief.

That relief passed almost as quickly as the second bolt that flamed through their vision, striking a tree off the side of the road and sending it toppling in their direction. "Run!" Gavin cried, and they all danced backward. But they never heard it fall.

They waited for a while, wondering if it was safe to continue, before Kaylyn finally deduced, "It must've gotten caught on another tree."

Gavin and Mallory weren't quite convinced by that explanation, still sure that the wood was waiting to crash down on them the moment they passed, but they could only stand in darkness for so long. They pressed onward without incident. Although, some-where deep down, it felt as though the tree was fol-lowing them.

"I think I have frostbite in my face." Mallory tapped at it with her free hand, but that, too, had gone numb.

"Try holding your umbrella in front of you as you walk," Gavin suggested, doing the same with his own, only to find himself blown back in the violence of the wind.

He crashed into Kaylyn along the way and she half-caught, half-pushed him to keep from both los-ing their footing.

"Honestly, there's no point in these things." Kaylyn chucked her umbrella to the side, off the road, with an eyeroll that none would see.

"Fair." Mallory followed suit.

Gavin held out for a moment, hoping for some way to harness the usefulness of the instrument, but after another brief blowback, he succumbed to the in-evitable and let the thing float away in the wind.

The farther they walked, the more winding the path became, and each took a turn slipping off the edge of the road, Gavin turning an ankle at one point and yelping out before walking it off, the cold numb-ing the pain quickly.

"Is there any chance," Mallory started, squinting into the road ahead, beyond the specks of water that masked everything beyond her glasses, "that we've already passed this guy's house and had no idea it was there?"

No one responded.

Finally, after a few more minutes of quiet, Mallory tried to break the silence again, if just for something to do. "So, let's say this isn't a ghost…"

"It's probably not," Kaylyn cut in, though she couldn't keep the word 'probably' out of her sentence, no matter how hard she tried.

"Okay, so, then, who do we think is doing all this?"

"It's definitely a ghost." Gavin attempted to nix the conversation, but Mallory persisted.

"But let's say it's not."

"That's not fair, I don't want to single anyone out falsely."

"They're not here to hear it. Unless you think it's one of us."

Gavin threw her an ironic side-eye, before realizing she would never know it had happened. "Fine. Then…I don't know…maybe Mick's not actually dead."

"Mick's dead, Gavin."

"You never know."

"I think Mav might tell you differently."

"Okay, then"—Gavin rolled his eyes and thought—"how about Mav? He's always been quiet and you never really know what he's thinking."

"Mav's a freaking saint," Mallory protested.

"Well, don't ask if you don't wanna hear my answer!"

"No, come on, I'm just saying," Mallory tried to save the conversation. "Kaylyn, how about you?"

She walked on for another moment, clapping watery soles against the hidden ground. "I think"—she chose her words carefully—"the most likely suspect is probably the person who's seemed least interested in spending time with us over the past day and a half."

"Irina talks a big game," Gavin noted, no interest in beating around the bush, "but do you really think she has it in her? She seems kinda…weak…"

"I can tell you from experience, she's not weak." Kaylyn unconsciously rubbed her shoulder, where Irina had grabbed her, earlier.

"Just because you think she's pretty doesn't mean she's incapable of hurting people," Mallory chided.

And Gavin was glad they couldn't see him go red. "I have a girlfriend," he murmured. "You know that."

"And she has a boyfriend. It's fine, Gavin, you don't have to get sheepish about it. She's obviously super beautiful," Mallory said, although Kaylyn scoffed behind her and she started to question her words. She was in too deep now and had to finish, though. "Like, no one would be surprised if *I* was the killer, because no one thinks I'm beautiful. It's because of the movies and perceptions."

"And gross male gaze-y stuff," Kaylyn inserted.

Gavin thought carefully for a minute before noting, "Don't say that about yourself. It's not true."

"Please, Gavin. Now's not the time for pep talks. You know what I mean; that's the point."

Gavin shrugged. "I don't know. Maybe…"

"Definitely," Kaylyn pronounced slowly.

"Who do you think is doing it, then?" Gavin turned to try to make Mallory out in the emptiness, but it was a futile endeavour.

For a bit, she said nothing. "I just—no…"

"Wait, what?" Gavin pressed. "You made us say."

She took a deep breath. "It's just, I can't help wondering whether…maybe this DJ guy is the one who's doing it."

Gavin and Kaylyn unconsciously slowed their paces, trying to push away the discomfort creeping into their stomachs.

Noticing the change in the already unpleasant air, Mallory offered, "I mean, probably not though…"

But before any of them could take the time to process the thought fully, they were struck by a speck of light in front of them, guiding them blurrily in the darkness toward a monstrosity in the distance.

They neared in silence and, without a word, they all stopped to take in the sight.

They had made it to DJ's house.

Alive.

18. Safety

"THEY'VE BEEN GONE a long time," Alyssa said, looking uselessly out the peephole in the front door, as though she could see anything but the grainy blur of the single streetlight through it.

"It'll be at least two hours," Travis reasoned. "Forty-five there, forty-five back. Presumably some time actually spent there."

"If they come back," Mav hummed, mostly to himself, but it was hard for everyone not to hear it.

"Don't say that," Malachi said shakily, looking down at a phone that was going to die at any moment. That didn't stop him from leaving it plugged into the worthless outlet.

Finally, Alyssa pulled herself away from the door and returned to the kitchen with a shiver. She wrapped her arms around herself before nuzzling in close to Travis for heat, avoiding, as best she could, his still-wet hair, from where he'd washed Brady's blood away. "Is anyone else really, really cold?"

"It's a little chilly," Mav conceded, fingering through the liquor bottles on the kitchen counter. He plucked a bottle of scotch from the rest. "Who the hell brought scotch?"

"Can I take a look at that?" Malachi held a hand out before examining the bottle closely. "This is good stuff, too."

"Probably Mick," Travis suggested. "Or Gavin. Gavin's weird enough to do that."

"Ours now." Mav shrugged, taking it back. He grabbed four rocks glasses in one hand and poured a finger of scotch into each. "To warm you up," he justified as he pushed one toward Alyssa before spreading the others around.

"Should we really be drinking, right now?" Malachi picked up his glass and eyed it carefully, tempted by the golden liquid but restrained by logic.

"It's always the right time to drink," Travis said forlornly, something he might've said in the previous life of five hours ago. He swigged it back and felt the comforting burn trickle down his throat. He breathed out heavily, between pleasure and pain, before coughing violently and grabbing against the counter for support.

"You don't…" Malachi began, before mumbling to himself, "shoot scotch…" He took a much more conservative sip and tried to enjoy the smoky caramel he sloshed around his mouth, but nothing tasted quite right, at the moment.

"Come on Mal, swig it back," Mav pressured, drinking his own in a single sip. "There's lots left for later."

"I just can't bring myself to do it."

"Suit yourself." Alyssa tapped the rim of her empty glass with a pink false fingernail, and Mav obliged with a slightly larger pour, this time.

"I should probably go check on Irina." Malachi rose, glass in hand, and felt his way through the darkness to the couch, where he oriented himself toward the stairs.

"Aw, screw her." Travis waved his hand dismissively, toying with his waistband as he returned to put an arm around Alyssa.

"Travis, be nice." Alyssa ran a hand down his back.

"Look, she doesn't want to be here…"

"She's just uncomfortable," Malachi justified.

"She wants to be alone, man. Let her be alone."

Malachi sat on the back of the couch, shaking his head, torn.

From down below, a quiet groan rose, undulating through the air in cold waves. As it passed them, it increased in volume. Higher, higher. Bleeding into a screech that chilled them all to the core.

Mav's hand tightened on his glass. Travis whipped around. Malachi shot up to face the stairs.

"That's what we heard." Alyssa threw back half her scotch, expression unchanged. "Last night. That's the ghost."

"It's not a ghost," Travis whispered. He'd meant to say it more definitively, but it wouldn't come out of his mouth any louder.

"Is that the boiler, Travis?" Alyssa still wouldn't turn around. There was no point.

"I have to go down and check on Irina," Malachi insisted forcefully. "I can't leave her down there with that thing."

The scream faded. Then returned.

"There *could* be a logical explanation," Mav reasoned.

"Gavin said you were possessed last night. Or, I'm pretty sure that's what he meant, anyway," Alyssa offered casually. "Saying some creepy things about running."

"I was probably talking in my sleep."

"So is she." Alyssa finally turned to face the stairs, looking on into the dark, expressionlessly. "Her sleep is just longer."

"I'm going down there," Malachi said, taking a few steps toward the stairs. "I don't care if any of you are coming with me." But they could hear, in his voice, that he cared.

"We'll come," Mav volunteered the rest, before leading them in the direction of the stairs.

"Wait." Travis stepped out in front, shuffle-stepping until he came into contact with Brady. Shaking his head, he shrugged and reached down, pushing the broken body and the rope that was still tied around its ankle away from the staircase. "All right, let's go."

The scream got no louder as they crept down the stairs, Travis' phone light the only guide in an otherwise black destination.

"Can we go a little faster?" Malachi pressed.

"I'm not falling down these stairs for Irina," Travis shot back.

At the bottom of the steps, he stopped and waited for the others. "Come on." Malachi headed in the direction of his and Irina's room. "Get the light over here."

But Travis was more concerned with the source of the wailing. "If she's the one screaming," he noted, pointing his light at the locked door, "then she's over there."

"It's not her," Alyssa muttered, but no one seemed to care.

Travis walked dazedly toward the mystery room, mind whirring, a slideshow of thoughts racing through his brain.

He grabbed the handle and tugged. Turned right, left. Nothing. The wail became more distant, as if it was running away from them and farther into the room.

"Maybe we can bust this thing down," Mav suggested, feeling the crack opposite the handle. "Too bad the hinges are on the inside."

"Maybe, if each of you guys take a run at it, one after the other…" Alyssa started.

Malachi cut her off. "You said this is what you heard last night, right? So, this is it. The ghost is in the closet. Great. Can we go check on my girlfriend, now?"

"Yeah, just a sec." Travis ducked down to examine the doorhandle, the bottom, trying to find a keyhole, anywhere.

"Not a sec, let's go now."

"All right, all right." Travis rose slowly. "We'll go now…"

The light on his phone went out.

"I thought your battery was at sixty percent," Alyssa breathed nervously. Travis said nothing in return.

"Run." Mav took the lead, clattering through the darkness.

Alyssa felt an arm smash into her side, but she couldn't make out who had bumped her. "Travis?"

she asked. "Travis!" Footsteps spun around her, clambered up the stairs, into the corners of the room.

She ran in the direction she was pretty sure led to the staircase and crashed violently into the side table between the locked door and the boiler room. She cursed as she spun to the ground and rolled onto her knees. Panting, she forced herself up, fire burning through her right leg. Then, something curled about her ankle and she smacked her head into the floor, hard.

Suddenly, the darkness became a friend.

19. Rundown

AT THE WOODEN steps to the front porch, Gavin, Mallory, and Kaylyn stopped, all thinking the same thing: *Can these hold our weight?*

If someone as massive as DJ could take these on a daily basis, then, surely, they could. But who was to say that he took this route to enter his house? Who was to say, frankly, that this even *was* his house?

Realistically, the place could have been abandoned, and could have been abandoned for years, and it would not have surprised them for a moment. Aside from the low light flickering from behind the picture window in front.

The rain was starting to fade and the darkness of actual night had taken over. Mallory cleaned the splotches on her glasses into streaks and smudges against her sopping wet shirt. The others squinted up at the crooked structure before them.

It was a tall house, much taller than The Little Maple Cabin. Squinting against the night and the rain, they could make out the pitched roof, inclined at an impossibly steep angle, of a kind no bird could safely perch upon. Shingles were missing in a wild, yet consistent, pattern, seeming to make abstract designs on the sides of the house. From what they could make out of the building's façade, the brick had been scarred by weather and, possibly, something much more violent. A windowpane was shattered, a widow's walk sat half unrailed, as the banister had cracked and, largely, wasted away.

The wraparound porch that might once have offered a calming view of the nature around was rife with shadows of varying degrees, suggesting holes that night attempted, futilely, to hide. It might have been more rickety than the back porch at the Cabin. Aside from the few hastily nailed-in plasterboards that offered a not-quite-heartening path to the front door.

Gavin was the first to take a hesitating step onto the first stair, pressing down a few times with his toe to make sure that it could take, at least, that much weight.

"No more than one person to a step at a time," he suggested, and was met with no arguments.

Even in the vacuum that seemed to suckle the sound out of everything, the creak of the step was painfully audible, like a person's back being snapped into pieces. All that was missing was the scream.

After taking the first two steps as slowly as he could, Gavin resolved that, if he were going to go through the wood, he would do so at any speed, and he pressed forward more quickly, in search of answers. He waited for the other two to join him at the chipped and splintery front door, and the moment they were near, he raised his fist, and knocked three times, slowly. Rap. Rap. Rap.

The door flung open, much too quickly, and DJ stood before them, as though he had been waiting for them to come. He was no longer wearing his black cloak, but he hardly looked comfortably attired for the evening. He was clad all in deep burgundy, in a suit replete with tails and a ruffled dress shirt. He could have been a welcoming butler for a fine dining event, if not for the harrowing grey eyes that bore into the souls of the guests.

And they were struck, once again, by just how tall he was. Too tall. Uncomfortably tall.

He blinked once as he stared down at them and, without a word, turned his back and strode into his house, leaving the door ajar.

Gavin, Mallory, and Kaylyn glanced at each other, not quite sure whether they should follow. But after coming all this way and enduring the hardships that had impeded their journey, there was no choice but to press onward. Gavin took a deep breath and stepped slowly inside.

Within, everything appeared to be *old*. A grandfather clock ticked and creaked near the front door, announcing the end of time. Cracked and eroded busts lined the walls, all in need of dusting. An antique shotgun hung upon a wall, seeming to point at the onlooker, wherever they may have stood. In the large room at the end of the hall, where DJ had just disappeared around the corner, a large portrait hung upon the wall, difficult to see in the minimal lighting. But it appeared to be the spitting image of DJ, just older by about fifteen years.

Half-expecting DJ to strike him dead the moment he entered the room at the end of the hall, Gavin approached with trepidation. But, inside, he found nothing but a perfectly safe, if gratuitously cavernous and sparsely decorated, room. A set of candles provided the light that flickered hauntingly, introducing them to shadows of varying shapes and sizes.

In the centre of the room sat DJ, resting with legs crossed in a large, burgundy armchair. He sipped lightly upon a glass of claret and would have seemed at peace, if not for the hard look in his eyes as he stared at the interlopers whom he may or may not have invited inside.

The respectful host, all the same, he gestured wordlessly to a couch across a coffee table from himself, and Gavin, Mallory, and Kaylyn felt impelled to accept his offer to sit.

Old, uncanny, and haunting, the inside of the house was, nonetheless, much nicer than its exterior. In theory, it could have been liveable, if not for the dust and cobwebs and museum décor.

DJ stared from one of them to the next, slowly, surveying their expressions, looking through them and into their minds. And during this exchange of kind, none dared to break the silence. DJ took a small but long sip from his glass before setting it down lightly upon the side table next to his chair.

He blinked slowly and, finally, he spoke. "I've been expecting you."

Mallory swallowed, speaking more to herself than to the room. "If your lights are out and our lights are out, how is that streetlight still on in front of the cottage?"

DJ returned an unsettling, almost reminiscent, smile. "That light never goes out."

Gavin swallowed. "The ghost?"

DJ eyed him up slowly, as if determining whether the young man was worthy of his approval, as if he sought for something deeper beneath the timorous exterior. No one dared speak during this silent assessment. Then, when he had concluded, DJ's uncanny eyes opened widely. "You've heard her, haven't you?"

Gavin nodded. "Yes. I mean, I think so…"

"They always come back," DJ mused. "Always. Come. Back."

"The ghosts?"

"No, the guests. You." DJ returned for a long sip of his claret. "Most think I'm jesting, when I mention the ghost. That, or they don't dare to know or believe. Some take it as a lark and don't fully listen, others come in search of advice for ridding themselves of the terror. And then"—he smirked slightly, in a manner much more unsettling than his normally expressionless face—"there are those who come to ream me out for allowing tenancy in such a perverse locale. Oh, they may write it all off as little more than a game I've played, a cruel trick. I've been reported to the local police on God-knows-how-many occasions. But they don't dare come up here anymore." His angular smile widened and his teeth appeared sharpened as tacks in the chasm behind his lips. "So, which one is it?"

"Which one is what?" Kaylyn was the only one of the three who could summon the confidence to speak, now.

"Your purpose, here? To chide me, condemn me? To seek salvation and explanations that, I fear, I cannot provide? Or—do you just want to know the story? Who doesn't love a good ghost story?"

"What the hell is happening in that house?" Gavin shook as he spoke, eyes flitting to the glass by DJ's side and suddenly craving anything alcoholic that could numb his mind.

"Hell, indeed," DJ commented, following Gavin's gaze. "Claret? Or, perhaps, tea? You seem fatigued after your walk."

It took everything Gavin had to decline, but he couldn't trust anything that came from this house or this giant man. "No. Thank you."

"Not for me." Kaylyn seemed to be thinking along the same line.

"That would really be…" Mallory started, eager for something warm, but with the smudges on her glasses starting to clear, she caught the warning expressions of her friends and sunk back in her chair, "…too much to ask of you."

DJ did not appear to take offence, but something in his eyes betrayed almost a pleasure at having impressed such a presence upon them. Gavin's mind shot back to Irina's sharp voice yelling, "…*one-star review for you!*", and he nearly broke out laughing, because this entire situation was so absurd. What came out instead was a squeaky twitter.

"Suit yourselves." DJ took another long, tempting sip. "Now, where were we?"

"The ghost," Gavin prodded with impatience. "Tell us what's going on in that house."

"My, my, we have been affected, haven't we? Well, where to begin?"

"The screaming. Who's screaming in the basement, behind the locked door? What's behind the door? Who's doing everything? How do we stop it? Who's Manny?"

"Well, those are quite a lot of places to begin. Shall we return to the beginning, then?" DJ rose, towering above them, and walked to the edge of the room, to where the painting hung upon the wall. He looked at it contemplatively as he began.

"As you may imagine, The Little Maple Cabin is quite old. Indeed, the name was not always such a misnomer as it is, today. When it was built, it was little more than a wooden shack. The decades passed and expansions were commissioned. Builders came and went and cursed their master, but none more so than Carlo Valentino. Some, say, one-hundred years ago, young Mr. Valentino arrived upon the grounds to service the will of Manuel Meadows, heir to a modest fortune and veritable recluse. He, and his wife Vera, had come out here to hide from the world in their wealth and comfort, purchasing the most remote location they could without disappearing from the world altogether. For there were still engagements to keep for the rich.

"She was of an unassuming kind, Vera. She had no passion for conversation, no love. But she served as an appropriate wife to a powerful man: quiet, pretty, forgettable but never forgotten. That was how Manuel liked, and that was how Manuel got. He'd long assumed that there was no passion within her. She was, simply, as she was. One whose life was sufficiently comforted by a book and the stability that he could provide.

"Mr. Valentino, by contrast, provided something much more. He awakened a fire within her that burnt bright. But as with all great fires, it was known for the damage it did, not for the length which it burned."

"They had an affair," Mallory concluded.

"To be crude, yes," DJ confirmed, still looking up at that disconcerting painting, as though he was deriving his tale from the lines and colours in the oil paint. "And who could blame her, really? Abandoned in her own home by the man who provided little more than a chequebook. He was a real man, and a young one; quite the contrast to the aging Manuel Meadows. And with a body firmer than a rock, if you believe the blabbermouthed Susies who've passed the tale down the generations. Shirt off all day in the blistering sun. How could she not find herself smitten?

"As for Mr. Valentino's perspective, who can say? Perhaps he was after money, notoriety, love, or simply pure, visceral sex. The man is lost to the ages and no one knows quite what became of him. The popular story—that Manuel killed him when he found out—for, of course, he found out—well, that's all tosh, if I may opine. He was a transient without a history and it's no shock he'd have even less of a future. Not that records were well-kept at the time, but surely he wouldn't have existed within any of them. The grounds have been searched, but no body found. He, simply, ceased to exist as quickly as he'd begun.

"But not before he cursed the place he touched. Upon learning that Vera would not run off with him, he swore an oath upon the grounds and declared that they would be, thenceforth, untenable for human life. That the house and the grounds around it should be a vacuum for death that repelled the living. That the only safety that could come to those who had passed, would be in pure and painful, eternal absence.

"Believe that, if you will. I tender my doubts."

"It's so quiet here," Gavin whispered. "That's why it's so quiet."

"It's quiet from the trees and the cold, my boy. Nought else."

"You, yourself, said there was a ghost out here, though."

"A ghost perhaps, the curse…well, that's a matter for later debate."

"So, who's haunting the grounds, then? Every ghost ever sucked into a vacuum?" Kaylyn scoffed but, at the sound, DJ tensed, still facing away, his back going hard. That had been a misstep that she would not dare make again.

"The story hardly ends there." DJ took a slow, loud breath, cocking his head slightly upward and taking in the face of the grey-eyed man up on the wall, so uncannily similar to him in everything but hair colour, and seeming to become him more and more as the moments ticked away. "Vera ran, when Manuel discovered her infidelity. None are quite sure to where, however. She disappeared, just as had her lover. Naturally, there were suspicions, but Old Manny denied them. He insisted that he had been chasing after her, attempting in futility to recover her faithfulness, to take her in the manner by which a man ought his wife, to demand a second chance. She was, he professed, his angel.

"I do believe that Manuel regretted his treatment of Vera when he found out. He was a cold and distant man, but not a bad one. Not a killer. Yet, his claim, that she evaded him within the Cabin, itself, and disappeared, as if through the wall—that was difficult for most to believe.

"He set off on a quest in search of her, at that point, braving the woods with a team of trusted acquaintances. He called, he cried out. He refused to return home until he had recovered her. For months he lived in those woods, camped out beneath trees that seemed to grow taller and quieter by the day. He could *smell* the death and decay pullulating in around him. He just failed to realize that they were his own.

"He was blinded, in his search: mauled by a bear that would have slaughtered him had it not been for the quick shot of a companion. And still, wounded, bleeding, eyes carved from his skull, he wrapped a bandage about his empty sockets and continued the search. His companions encouraged that he rest, return to his home and make life of what little survival he had left in his bones. But he spurned them, one and all. And though they were loath to leave a blind man, crawling alone about the forest floor, his attitude had become obsessive and his temperament foul. One by one they returned to their homes while Manuel Meadows carried on about his search.

"No one quite knows what became of him from there. Logic would suggest that he plunged over the cliff or was eaten for his troubles, but no body nor bone has been found. As the story goes, he still haunts The Little Maple Cabin, blindfolded, hunting for Vera—his angel—wherever she may be. Drawn to women of the meek and angelic sort, whom he mistakes for his wife; repulsed and spiteful of men who impede his potential for love, again."

"And that's why he kills," Gavin concluded the story.

"Kills?" DJ turned to face them, his eyes as hollow as ever, but his expression somehow troubled. "I never said he kills."

"You said no one'd survived more than one night in that house in decades," Gavin prodded.

"You mistake me." DJ strode two steps forward, his monstrous size reminding the others that it was best not to contradict him. "I stated that no one had *stayed* more than one night in that house in decades. They heard screaming in the night, saw their friends crying out in their sleep, some even swear they've seen Old Manny, himself, coming for them with the speed of one who could see through the blindfold that still wraps around his missing eyes.

"But he's never killed."

Gavin glanced to a blanched Kaylyn and a sickly Mallory. "He's killing now."

DJ took a moment to process, the candles behind him flickering his figure into larger and sharper shapes and sizes. Finally, he spoke slowly, considering his words. "How many people have died?"

"Four. Assuming nothing's happened since we've been gone."

"If Manuel has taken to killing, then you must leave the house, at once. There is no precedence for this and I cannot say what he would do. But if you ask for my opinion, I don't believe the entity you're dealing with is one of supernatural origins. Simply put: Manny wouldn't kill for sport."

"So, you think it's one of us," Kaylyn confirmed.

"I do hope so. For if Manny's taken a murderous tack, there's no telling where, or how, he may be stopped. Have you called for the police?"

"We tried," Gavin noted, "but the power's been out."

"It's the same here, I'm afraid." He paced slowly to the front window and examined the weather beyond the black. "The storm is picking back up. I can drive into town when it clears away, but my car is old and I don't suspect she'd survive this weather."

"One of us went to try to find the police."

"Then I hope, for his sake, the roads are kind. To the unfamiliar, they seem to wind themselves into knots that were never there before. Even I've fallen victim to their tricks, and I've lived here for most of my life, since we returned."

"Returned?" Mallory couldn't stop herself from asking.

"Indeed." DJ turned from the window and faced them, face half-shadowed in the fading candlelight. "When my grandmother heard what had happened, she returned to an England she hadn't known since she was a babe. On her death, my mother discovered the property deed, still in our name and, to save on expenses, returned us to this place at once."

"What are you saying?" Gavin felt his palms go cold as DJ crossed the room, once again, and stopped beside the haunting portrait, this time looking out upon his guests so that the resemblance was painfully striking.

"I'm saying," DJ boomed, "that my great-grandfather, Manuel Meadows, has been watching over you since you arrived."

20. Pursuit

ALYSSA WAS NOT out for long. Or, at least, she didn't think she was. The swarm of darkness that engulfed her in the basement did nothing to suggest the time, nor were any sounds present in the house to indicate movement, action, or life.

Or, maybe that was just her ears. As she came to, she became aware of footsteps and thuds, a distant grunt, the sound of something falling, the crash of something shattering.

She pushed hard off the ground, trying to get onto her knees, then to her feet. But the first contact of her toes with the ground sent her wobbling to her right and down hard into a side table, shoulder-first, her head barely escaping a second concussion.

She was slower in her attempt to rise, this time. Pausing on her knees, even as the dread and adrenaline crept back inside her stomach and cried out to RUN! Eyes closed so tightly that her lids started to ache, she took a deep breath, then another. There was no good in opening her eyes. There was nothing to see, either way.

Her ankle threatened to turn, no matter at which direction she angled her foot, but she focussed, this time, until she found it flat on the ground. She clutched at the side table for balance, but a searing pain through her shoulder made her release immediately.

Something shifted behind her. Malachi's voice screamed something from a distance, but whether it was words or pain, she could not be certain.

Reaching across her body with her good arm, she pretzeled herself awkwardly until she'd managed some form of stability. There would be no way to get both of her feet flat whilst crouching. She would be down again a moment later. Tensing, sweat beads—or were they blood beads?—burning on her forehead, she forced herself up in the air with a whimpering cry.

"Hah." She breathed a pained sigh of relief as she wobbled, but did not fall. Both hands collapsed down on the table but the pain in her shoulder nearly crumpled her, again.

"Focus, focus, focus," she whispered to herself, heartbeat thudding into her stomach and threatening to expel scotch and mimosas across the floor.

There was shuffling above her. The scream in the closet recommenced. "GO AWAY! GO AWAY!" she cried out, tears starting to flow into her eyes.

Breath almost gone from her body, she lurched as hard as she could toward the staircase—or, where she thought the staircase to be.

As she plunged through the darkness, the air cut at her face, stale and cold. She stutter-stepped, stumbled. Felt as though something was grabbing at her ankle. She just, barely, shook it away. It was still behind her, though. She knew that *something* was still behind her.

She turned right and collided with a bottom step, much closer than she'd expected it to be. Now, the tears started to roll down her cheeks, although she fought to suppress the yell that burned in her gut.

Crashing up the steps, she felt blood beginning to trickle down her leg, her jeans sticking painfully to the cut that she knew would only hurt more when she reached safety. If she reached safety. She was halfway up now, and a vague outline of night light beckoned, just the hazy fingers of the streetlight out front, calling her.

But she was equally called back down, the unseen and impossible sensation behind her seeming to follow, its gravitational pull thick, potent. Her body shuddered, her back sweated in pellets of ice. Her bad shoulder smashed into the wall and the pain nearly froze her, but her legs fought through. Mostly. The pain, combined with whatever drew her back, had her running in slow motion, her light and wispy body feeling thousands of pounds, as if she had anvils tied to her ankles.

"Travis!" she called out through tears that had soaked down to her collar and were starting to weigh down her clothes. "Travis!"

Her foot hit the top step and she flew up like a shot, the pressure from behind relieved in an instant. She was free, though still blinded in the electrically depowered night. Alyssa flailed her arms about herself, still running at the fastest pace she could manage, but she didn't prepare for the wall before her.

With a hard crash, she bounded against something large and hard, sending her bouncing back toward the stairs. And she likely would have fallen if the mass before her hadn't thrown its arms out and grabbed her by the neck. "No!" she screamed, feeling the pressure there, not yet squeezing but able to begin at any moment.

She beat her fists out at the creature and felt them bound uselessly off hundreds of pounds of flesh, blood, and bone. "Get away from me! Get off of me!" She tried to punch at its head, but her arms were too short and it held her at a distance. "Travis! Travis!"

"Shh, shh! Calm down, calm down," the creature's voice whispered in a suspiciously familiar tone. The large hands loosened from around her neck and slid down to the front of her chest, holding her at bay lest she continue her violent assault. "It's me," he said. "It's Malachi. Don't attack."

Slowly, Alyssa's heart began to slow as her arms decompressed as if the air was slowly being released from within. "Malachi," she repeated, feeling better to hear the name aloud once more. "Malachi." Squinting through the distant light, the faintest edges of his face began to come into focus. "Where's Travis? Where're the others?"

"I don't know, I don't know." Malachi lowered his hands, as well, now that the threat had passed. "I think Irina's still downstairs. I wanted to go to her, but in the panic I just wanted to get outta the basement. Travis and Mav, I have no idea."

Footsteps crashed along the hall, accompanied by a crack of thunder, albeit a much more distant one than those they'd become accustomed to. Malachi and Alyssa both turned to face the oncoming sound and managed to make out the long hair of Travis, out of breath and hunched over a bit at the waist.

"Travis!" Alyssa ran to him and wrapped her arms around him, breathing in sweat and fear. She could feel how quickly his heart still beat, the shake of his body beneath hers. "Travis, are you okay?"

"Y-yeah," he choked, shaking his head. "I'm fine. Just…" He processed for a moment, looking back over his shoulder uselessly. "Didn't know where you were. I was looking."

"I think I passed out downstairs," Alyssa explained, keeping her bad arm wrapped around Travis as she raised the good one to her head and felt around for blood. "How long was I out?"

"Can't've been more than a couple of minutes," Malachi suggested, but he didn't sound convinced, as though the entire ordeal had warped his ability to process time. "Maybe a couple more than that," he murmured.

Travis just shook his head.

"There *is* a ghost in here." Alyssa looked from one to the other, knowing that, even though they could not see the forcefulness in her eyes, they would still be able to feel the depth of her gaze upon them.

"It…does feel that way," Travis conceded.

"I need to go check on Irina." Malachi looked toward the stairs but couldn't bring his legs to move in the necessary direction.

"Do you know where Mav is?" Alyssa looked up at Travis. She was starting to settle, but he still seemed skittish.

"No." He checked over his shoulder again. "Haven't seen him."

A flicker of movement caught Alyssa's eye over Travis' left shoulder and her heart stopped, just as time slowed. The vision was accompanied by a crash that seemed to shake the foundation of the house.

The instinct to run in the opposite direction conflicted with the need to know what stood before them, looming in the doorframe. Travis led the rush before either of the other two had had time to process.

Alyssa lurched forward as Travis wrenched out of her grasp. Malachi must not have seen her in his path, and his hip sent her spinning on the way past. Grabbing the banister at the top of the stairs, she just managed to remain upright, although her good shoulder took a hard yank in the process.

She was the last to arrive at the entrance, where dark figures threatened to enter, silhouetted in the streetlight. But as she neared, her heart slowed, along with her breath. It was just Gavin, Mallory, and Kaylyn, finally having returned from their long walk into the night.

"You guys are lucky you missed it." She breathed out, no time for even a 'hello'.

But none of them responded to her greeting. They just stood there, transfixed by something in the corner of the room. In fact, Travis and Malachi were equally fixated. No one moving, no one speaking.

Mouth still hanging slightly open, Alyssa turned slowly to face their collective direction. It was hard to make out in the faded orange light, but it was bright

enough that there could be no doubt of what lay before them.

Mav's head was propped up against the baseboard
and his legs sprawled out in front of him. One arm
rested over his chest and the second was bent behind
his back, broken in two by brute force. His eyes were
closed, as if he was sleeping. And he could have been.

If not for the long, jagged and messy slice across
his throat, just beneath his gaping mouth, still gushing
a slow but steady trickle of blood down his chest and
soaking through his shirt.

21. Determination

THE DOOR SLAMMED shut behind the trio and the clattering sound shocked everyone into action. They rushed, in unison, toward Mav's crumpled body, a small piece of them hoping to find salvageable life beneath the certain death, the more logical parts of their clustered minds just begging for a clue that could lead to the end of the madness.

Travis dropped down to his knees by the body while Gavin flew to his close friend's other side. Mallory sputtered, "No, no, this can't be happening. No!" as Kaylyn and Malachi blew past Alyssa, one on either side, nearly sending her to the ground, yet again.

"He's dead," Gavin announced, uselessly, hating himself for needing to say it, but also not believing it could possibly be true until he heard it aloud.

"But he was such a saint," Malachi blubbered, lip quivering. "He was the one. The one person who least deserved to die."

"He was a good friend," Travis concurred. "But no matter how good we are, nothing can save us from this thing. Clearly."

"You think it was the ghost?" Gavin looked up at him, surprised at this sudden change in attitude.

"We heard things, while you were gone. The screaming. I can't see how it could be anything else at this point." He looked from Gavin to where he thought Alyssa stood to his left. "You guys were right."

"Only problem is," Kaylyn cut in sharply, "our creepy as hell host just told us that the ghost has never killed before. And he seems pretty sure it wouldn't just go on a killing spree for the sake of it."

They all turned to look at her, no one wanting to pose the question that she was waiting for them to ask. All of them knowing the answer, already.

Before they could get to the end of that thought, however, a loud screech burst through the house, startling them and turning all heads toward the front door.

Mallory, still standing next to the entrance, threw the door open wide, the wind catching it and sending it sailing into the wall at full force, yet again. Alyssa, Kaylyn, and Malachi stepped forward to join Mallory by the door while Gavin and Travis slowly took to their feet.

Outside, Dorian's car slid wildly in the rain. With a hard flick of the wheel, he flew to a stop just a few feet from the front of the house, and stepped out into the storm, almost before the engine had shut off.

"Dorian, where are the police?" Alyssa cried out, desperately searching in the distance for flashing lights or sirens.

Pulling his wool coat tightly around himself to guard against the lighter, but still consistent rain, he jogged the few steps up to the front door, glancing back over his shoulder to verify that he'd shut the door before leaving his car behind.

Finally inside, he threw the coat off quickly and ran a hand through his slick blonde hair, one of the few things that still gleamed brightly in the otherwise empty night.

"Tell me someone's coming," Kaylyn nearly commanded of him. "Dorian. Tell me!"

He shook his head. "Nothing."

"What do you mean, 'nothing'?" Gavin stepped forward, eyes wide.

"I got into town," Dorian began before looking around at the group that had rushed him and left him imprisoned on the front door mat. "Two of you are missing. Where are they? What happened to not splitting up?"

A few averted their gazes, but Travis, despite his general agreement with the original plan, defended the actions of the group on their behalf. "We made the choices that needed to be made. Irina is downstairs. And, honestly, who cares?"

"Hey!" Malachi tensed, but no one cared to listen.

"And Mav?" Dorian pressed, sounding almost frustrated.

"Mav is dead," Gavin pronounced the words slowly, allowing the full impact to seep into the room, yet again.

For a moment, Dorian stared at Gavin, disbelieving, confused. His brow furrowed and his mouth hung slightly open.

Finally, he took a long blink and shook his head. "W-well, that's..." He breathed deeply. "That's really too bad. Didn't know him that well, but he seemed like one of the good ones."

"He was a saint," Malachi repeated, tears coming to his eyes.

"So, please." Kaylyn laid a hand on Dorian's shoulder, the water that soaked her blouse dripping onto Dorian's jeans, though he decided against commenting on it at a time of such desperate tragedy. "Tell us that the cops are on their way."

Dorian pursed his lips and looked around at the group forlornly. Even in the dark, they could tell. There was nothing he needed to say.

"I drove into town. Honestly, I don't know how I got there. Got lost a few times. I'd swear the roads seemed to change directions on me."

"DJ said they do that," Gavin noted and Dorian looked confused.

"We'll explain after," Kaylyn silenced him, impatiently. "Go on."

Dorian continued, "Anyway, I got into town and the place was dead." He caught himself. "Sorry, bad word to use. But it was empty. Didn't see a single living soul. I drove up and down the street, looking for the police station, or even for someone I could ask where the station was. Got nothing. Finally found the place hidden off the edge of town, but it was closed down."

"Closed?" Kaylyn snapped. "When the hell is a police station ever *closed*?"

"That's what I said." Dorian shook his head. "I swear. I pounded on that door, went around the back. Everything was dark. I don't know. Maybe a two-person operation in a small town with no crime doesn't feel the need to keep their doors open twenty-four-seven. Or maybe they were out dealing with something. Who knows? Either way, I tried and got nowhere. So, I drove around awhile looking for a place where I could use a phone. But, I'm telling you, the entire place was shut down like no one lived there, anymore.

"I started driving back, trying to get to the next town down the way, but the GPS crapped out on me and it took me forever just to find the main road again. Honestly, it's a good thing we're in the middle of nowhere or I probably would've crashed the car a few dozen times just trying to stay on the road. If I'm being honest with you, I don't even know how I made it back here, alive."

Gavin fell back against the wall behind him and crunched into a seated position. Mallory lowered her head. Malachi continued crying and was joined, to a less exaggerated extent, by Alyssa. Kaylyn collapsed with her arms around Dorian, shaking her head. "This can't be. It can't be."

Dorian waited a moment and let her let her anger out, but when enough time had passed, he gently lifted her away and looked her deep in the eyes. "Can I take a look at Mav?"

With a swallow, she nodded slowly and led him to the corner of the room. Dorian bent down on one knee and inspected the body. He shook his head. "Crude work. Not like the others. I'd say he put up a pretty good fight."

"But he still lost," Gavin spat sickly from his place on the floor. "And we're all going to lose as long as we stay in this house with that thing."

"Gavin, you heard what DJ said," Kaylyn insisted forcefully. "This isn't a ghost. This is a *person*."

Gavin tensed and stood up, fire in his eyes. "I really don't give a damn one way or the other. At this point, the only way we're safe is if we're not here. I say we all go sit in the car until morning. Who's with me?"

"There still aren't enough seats for all of us in the one car." Kaylyn tensed, frustrated.

"Then we break windows of the others. I don't care. It's just somewhere to spend the night that's not here, so at least we, maybe, have a chance of making it 'til morning."

He started toward the door, but Dorian took his shoulder, not gently, but not roughly, either. "Gavin, take it easy," he advised. "We're all scared, but there's no good in rushing off on your own. We've gotta do things logically."

"Logic went out the window when we booked a haunted house for the weekend."

"Forget the damn ghosts, Gavin." Kaylyn took his shoulders from Dorian and looked him hard in the eyes, seeking the brain behind the irises and trying to impress reality upon him. "We all know who did this. Maybe we don't want to believe it. Maybe it doesn't fit our narrative of being a big happy work family who all love each other unconditionally. But we *know*. And it wasn't a ghost."

"We don't know," Gavin muttered, trying to pull his eyes away, if nothing else.

"But we do." Kaylyn held nothing back now, pushing Gavin aside and taking control of the room. "Who's the one person who's had no alibi this entire time? Who's made a point of being by herself so none of us could possibly know where she actually was at any given moment?"

"No!" Malachi growled. "Don't say it!"

"You know it's true!" Kaylyn spat. "She never liked any of us. She's the only one of us with motive and she's had all the opportunity in the world."

"Take it back! You take it back *right now!*" He tried to block her path as Kaylyn pushed by and headed toward the staircase. But he stopped short of physically grabbing her. "Take it back." His voice became weaker.

Mallory followed on instinct and Dorian followed suit. Travis took Alyssa around the shoulder and guided her slowly back toward the depths she had so recently escaped, stroking her shoulder gently to comfort her, not realizing just how much that hurt. Gavin remained glued to the doorstep for a few moments longer, wanting nothing more than to break free from this prison and take solace in anywhere-but-here. But being left alone seemed worse and he grudgingly brought up the rear.

Kaylyn's phone was nearing death, but she'd saved enough power for this sneak attack.

"The light's gonna go out," Alyssa whimpered. "Like Travis' did." But Kaylyn wasn't listening, nor did she have any interest in hearing that story at the moment. She pressed forward, possessed, until she had the entire group standing in a semicircle around Irina's door.

"Last chance." Malachi's lip shook as he pleaded. "We can just walk away and pretend none of this ever happened. And she doesn't have to know what you think of her."

"Malachi, I'm sorry." She looked at him hard, unapologetically. "But it doesn't matter how many times I take it back, or any of us takes it back. Because, we all know."

There was no argument left to be made. Malachi went silent and faded to the back of the group.

Kaylyn turned to the door, rage replacing every anxious thought that had overtaken her body over the past day. She pounded with all her might, powerfully enough that a stronger person might have put a fist through the door. "Irina, open up!" she demanded. "Open up, *right now!*"

The door flung open and Irina stood before them, wearing just a long shirt and a murderous glare to accompany clenched teeth and a pulsing vein in her neck.

"What do you want?" she demanded, violently, fixed exclusively upon Kaylyn. It took her a moment to realize that the pair of them were not alone and that she was not being challenged to a duel. And it took her a moment longer to realize that everyone had their eyes focussed upon her right arm.

She lowered it quickly, but it was too late.

They had all seen the paring knife, brandished recklessly in her hand.

22. Democracy

SLOWLY, THEY ALL stepped back, though Kaylyn did so with an aggressive posture still angled at Irina. "Well?" Irina snapped, irritably, but her eyes betrayed her sheepishness at having been caught.

"See?" Kaylyn pointed at the knife as if no one had noticed. "What did I tell you?" She jabbed her finger at the weapon emphatically, a few more times. "She's the one. She's the one who's been doing this all along."

Irina's hand flinched, as if to bring the knife up. If she struck now, she'd surely be overpowered, but not before she'd had the chance to plunge the blade through Kaylyn's chest. But as her eyes flitted about the room, she thought better of vengeance and opened her hand, allowing the knife to drop to the floor with a clatter, landing just inches from her bare foot. The sound sent Gavin jumping and Mallory grabbing at Kaylyn's shoulder, trying to extract her from the epicentre of danger. But Kaylyn shrugged her off, still glaring fiercely at her foe.

"You are an empty-headed little girl." Irina blew air hard from her nose. "You think you are important and knowledgeable. But you are little more than a petty instrument. You make loud noise, but you are easy to be played."

"We all saw it. You're finished, you bitch."

Irina scoffed. "You saw nothing as there was nothing to see. You interrupt me in my peace and you come with accusations. Unfounded. You are pathetic!" She spat on the floor.

"Murder weapon in hand and you still deny it. You really are a piece of work." Kaylyn stepped forward, suddenly confident in her ability to take Irina down, now that the knife was on the floor, though her eyes flitted to it as a backup plan, and she wondered if, maybe, with a quick lunge…

"What murder weapon? The pothead fell from rope. The sleepy one had head chopped by a blade sharper than this one. Your brother and his *friend* were bashed by rocks. Tell me, what did my little knife do?"

Kaylyn's eyes burned fire. "You killed Mav."

Irina blinked once, taking in this information. This time, she proceeded more carefully with her words, speaking slowly, in a less jagged tone. "I did not like the quiet one, but I did not know he was dead until this minute. I have not been from this room since I came down here, and he was, then, still alive."

"Then explain the knife." Although she was burning with rage and wearied by sadness, Kaylyn still managed a sadistic smile at the prospect of making Irina squirm, of putting her on the spot and driving in the metaphorical dagger. She even took a small step forward, angling her body to appear larger, though she was still a fraction of Irina's size.

But Irina did not squirm. She remained motionless, calm. "I took it from kitchen for self-defence. I have not used it. It has sat in my hand in case the killer comes for me. Nothing more. Nothing less."

"Okay, Kaylyn." Malachi stepped forward, hands raised in a pacifying stop sign. "I think we've taken this far enough. We *know* Irina can't've done this. She's been down here the whole time. There isn't even any blood on the knife."

All eyes, less Kaylyn's, turned upon the blade and simultaneously acknowledged that, sure enough, the stainless steel glinted fresh silver in the cell phone's light. Irina's expression turned from defensive to triumphant as she turned her chin up at Kaylyn smugly. "Pathetic," she whispered once again.

"She cleaned it." Kaylyn didn't miss a beat, never taking her eyes off the woman before her.

"Isn't there a way we can check that?" Gavin piped up, hoping to end the ordeal as quickly as possible.

Travis responded dryly, "Do you have a blacklight and a DNA kit handy?"

Gavin reintegrated himself into the crowd with head bowed. Malachi aided his disappearance by pushing forward to the front of the crowd. Though he began gruffly, ready to fight to protect his beloved, when he reached the fray, he got cold feet and stared on awkwardly from a few steps away. "This whole thing: there's no reason for it. Can't we just drop it?"

"No," Kaylyn fired back, "she's guilty as hell. Think about it." She appealed to the room at large. "She's spent all weekend avoiding us, without an alibi. And she and Mav had a fight, just this morning."

"Only one so petty and selfish as you would think a dispute over pie and booze would constitute motive."

Kaylyn ignored the interruption. "We know she doesn't like us much, what better chance to pick us off one by one than during a weekend in the middle of nowhere."

For a moment, there was silence, as everyone let the prosecution's closing argument settle in, while, at the same time, waiting eagerly for the defence's rebuttal.

Finally, Irina shook her head. "You are right about one thing: I do not like you." Malachi held his face in his hand. "But it is little wonder," she continued, "when you throw about your false accusations with no proof. I do not have time for you." She turned back to her room and moved to shut the door behind her, but Kaylyn shot her foot in the way.

"Where d'you think you're going?"

"Away from this…this…absurdity."

"You killed my friend. You think that's *absurd?*"

"I did nothing and you know this. But you cannot bear to think that you are wrong!"

Kaylyn took a harsh step toward Irina and Malachi stepped in between the feuding women. "Okay, let's not get carried away. There's no reason to think…"

But both ignored him. "You are dishonourable. You believe only in that which suits you and the rest is to be ignored. You act like queen, but beneath is knave."

"Just admit it. There's no point in lying at this point."

"Fine, I admit it. I am killer. But I killed only one person: you." Irina lunged forward and Malachi attempted to block her, but Kaylyn sidestepped him and dove in, low, at Irina's knees. This would've taken her to the ground if Kaylyn hadn't misjudged the angle in the flicker of light as her phone fell to the floor. Kaylyn crashed hard into the doorframe and Irina laughed as she grabbed Kaylyn's long, black hair, dragging her back and wrapping a forearm about her neck.

At this, Dorian leapt forward to drag Irina away, but was met with Malachi, who easily brushed the smaller man aside. Also disapproving of the kerfuffle, Malachi took Irina's waist and, gently, pulled her away from Kaylyn, though this was not so gentle upon Kaylyn's neck, which flew back at the initial momentum.

"EVERYONE STOP!"

And, for the second time that day, Irina and Kaylyn were frozen, mid-battle, by a call for attention. This time, it was Gavin who commanded the room, although he shook at the sight of all those eyes upon him. It was too late to turn back now, however. "This isn't getting us anywhere." He swallowed hard. "So, I say, we handle this the only way reasonable people do: democratically. Anyone have a problem with that?"

A few glances were exchanged, some hesitations. But no one dared break the silence. Gavin took a few slow, deep breaths, waiting for someone, anyone, to take the floor. But no one did.

"Okay. Then we vote. Who thinks Irina is innocent?"

Malachi's hand shot up immediately, his face scanning the crowd for further support. Irina, in distaste for the venture, instinctively refused to participate, at first, until the weight of her fate finally impelled her to raise a slow but deliberate hand high into the air. Amongst the rest, eyes turned about, facing the floor, the ceiling, the walls. But no further hands were raised.

"All right." Gavin shook a little as he prepared for the inevitable. "Who thinks Irina is guilty?"

Kaylyn voted confidently, a smug smile on her face. Mallory followed her lead and Dorian, with a slow breath, allowed his hand to rise, as well. Travis and Alyssa shared a long look from across the room before both raised their hands in unison.

Gavin breathed a sigh of relief that he would not have to break a tie. "All right then. The people have spoken."

"Hey!" Malachi protested. "The jury has to be unanimous."

"Let it go," Travis advised, not impolitely. "This isn't court; this is life and death. No one cares about technicalities."

"Guys," he pleaded, but no one cared to listen.

"Now what?" Alyssa looked to Gavin for answers.

Gavin realized, suddenly, that, although he'd always expected Irina to lose the vote, the thought of what to make of that had barely crossed his mind. "Um…" He gritted his teeth.

"There must be some rope in the garage." Travis saved him. "Alyssa and I will go to look." Alyssa flinched at being volunteered for the job, but she preferred it to the alternative of letting Travis out of her sight, again. "The rest of you"—he bit his lip in thought. "Take her upstairs, to the kitchen. Easier to keep an eye on her up there. Brighter, at least."

"Sounds good to me." Kaylyn nodded once, but emphatically.

"No," Malachi tried, once again. "Guys, you're making a mistake."

Travis ignored him, passing by to place a hand on Alyssa's back and guide her to the stairs. "Gav, lend me your phone." Gavin complied and Travis lit the way.

"Come on," Malachi attempted again.

Dorian moved in close, speaking quietly so as not to make Malachi feel as though he was on display. "You can't win this fight," he advised. "It's better not to fight the group or you might find yourself being next." He didn't speak with malice, but the words rang clearly. "It's better to comply. If she's not guilty, we'll know soon enough."

"Back away, follower." Irina took a step at him, but Malachi held her back, brain still running at violent speeds.

Malachi breathed deeply. "I can't see any other way."

"No!" Irina screamed out, covering her mouth in embarrassment at the outburst. She closed her mouth quickly and thought for a moment before placing a hand upon Malachi's arm and whispering softly, "You can't let them do this to me. You know it is not true."

"I know." He looked at her sadly. "I know it's not. But I think…Dorian's right. We can't prove it. We don't have a choice, right now."

"You must protect me."

"I will!" Malachi exclaimed with concern. "I really will, I promise! I won't let them do anything to you. I'll keep an eye on you as often as I can. But we have to go with the will of the group until they learn they're wrong."

"How dare you!" She stepped at him, but he held her back easily in his massive hands.

"Please," he said, tears welling in his eyes. "This isn't easy for me, either. I don't want this to happen but…"

"But you are coward! You do not fight for what is good and right."

"Okay," Kaylyn cut in with an eye roll. "We've heard enough out of you. Let's get her upstairs."

"I will go nowhere with you!"

"Come on," Malachi prodded softly. "There's no good in making this hard."

"This is injustice!"

"No one cares what you think," Mallory interjected in defence of Kaylyn more than in support of her own opinion.

Gavin stepped forward. "The vote has spoken." He took a spot behind Irina, and Mallory shifted to do the same. Kaylyn reached a hand out to guide Irina forward, but found it swatted viciously away. At that, Dorian stepped in with a violent shove, sending Irina bucking forward.

Irina turned her shoulder and her arm swung back, as if in preparation to strike, but Malachi caught her before she could commit any provable act of violence. "Let's go," he advised her, guiding her to the stairs in front of the group.

When they reached the top of the stairs, with difficulty, they were greeted by the slamming of the garage door as Travis and Alyssa returned, silhouetted against the black, but with a long rope in hand. "I'm pretty sure we've got enough to wrap her around about ten times over," Travis noted.

"Let's get this over with." Gavin pursed his lips.

"I'm not taking any part in this." Malachi stepped back from his girlfriend as Travis and Alyssa approached with the rope, Gavin, Kaylyn, Dorian, and Mallory following closely behind.

"I will not let you…" Irina began, but she didn't have much choice in the matter, as her slight figure was overpowered by the rest with ease, the ropes tied tightly around her arms, ankles, edges, and angles. The guilt and discomfort mandated by the process led them to work in silence, tying her off at various spots with no logic or reason.

She cried out as the thick rope pulled her chest, tightly, leading Gavin to offer the only words spoken during the unsettling process: "Don't strangle her."

When, finally, they were done, she was dressed so excessively in rope that she could have survived a Siberian winter.

They stepped away, but could not admire their work. They were sick at what they had done, even if they knew it was right.

"I think we should leave the room," Gavin finally managed. "To protect her pride."

"You lie to yourself all you want, but you know what you have done!" Irina spat out. "You will all die in this house, but it will not be because of me. It will be your own fault. Every one of you."

Shaking sickly, they backed out of the room, in the direction of Kaylyn and Dorian's bedroom.

"You are all cursed, if I should die here! You leave me to be taken, but you will come to regret your mistake. I will return! I will return to haunt you all until your final, dying day. And I will not stop until you have felt the pain of what you have done! Do you hear me? I do not care. It does not matter if you listen, for your fate will be the same. You will regret this. I swear upon the death of my grandmother. You will regret this. You—all of you—

"You will all die here!"

23. Light

THEY SAT IN a makeshift circle around the edges of the bed, backs to each other, but heads instinctively turned to face the middle. The window that looked out onto the backyard provided the only light, and even this was fleeting on a nearly moonless night. A few stars pretended to light the way, perhaps. But no matter how adjusted their eyes had become to seeing nothing at all, most features and figures were invisible.

Travis squinted through the black in search of Alyssa's face, right next to him. He could ask Gavin to turn on his light, he supposed, but there was no good in wasting power for the sake of comfort. There were hours until sunrise and very few battery hours left on the phones that survived.

Travis was glad to be seated on the window side of the room, at least, where he could grasp at the minimal luminescence that pretended to shine in. But, more importantly, where he could keep an eye on the door. It may have been out of sight, but at least he would be the first to know if anyone came through it. Or any*thing.*

From beyond the door, Irina continued to scream out obscenities and threats, but her words were muffled into little more than a consistent din.

"Her throat's going to be so sore for the next three days," Malachi noted, concern in his voice.

"That's a problem for the police to deal with."
Travis didn't have time for tact. He much preferred
the silence, where he could hear if anything were
coming down the hall, ready to take them all.

"You know this doesn't make sense, right, guys?"
Malachi tried to reason for the millionth time. "If
you're all so convinced Irina did this, why're we all
hiding in a bedroom when she's tied up?"

In case we're wrong, Kaylyn thought, but she didn't
want to admit to the possibility, so the room remained silent.

Travis' hand sought Alyssa's but came up with little more than cold bedsheets. He swiped around
against the mattress for a few moments until he con-
tacted skin. From there, he followed the trail to the
warmth of her flesh.

"I love you," she whispered in his ear, not caring
if anyone else could hear.

"I love you more," he replied, pulling himself in
close, now that he'd identified her warmth amidst the
bodies.

"No, you don't." She nuzzled her long, pink hair
against his cheek and felt *almost* safe for the first time
since the previous afternoon.

"Yes, I do," he insisted. "You saved me. You
know that. I was going nowhere until you set me
right. Your family—everything you've done for me. I
don't even know how to say it."

"You've said enough. Anyway, it's not the words
that matter." She moved her hand to his thigh and
stroked it lightly, taking in every fibre of his jeans.

He kissed the top of her head and left his mouth against her hair, breathing in the remnants of the strawberry shampoo that had since bled into sweat and daily oil.

Travis lifted his hand gently across her body, from her hard yet fragile kneecap up her hip, her side, to her soft, smooth cheek.

Pulling back, he curled her face upward so that he could face her properly, taking in her beauty in the dark and savouring a world where neither of them had to live in fear or doubt. Though he could barely make her out, his mind filled in the blanks, projecting before him a picture of truth and innocence, love and perfection. A tiny sliver of light offered a glimpse of her nose and mouth, hinting at the bag under her right eye.

But the moment of purity could not be allowed to last in this house. And, the moment that Travis began to feel that nothing could hurt them, so long as they stuck together, the tiny glimmer of features across Alyssa's face began to flicker.

A dark image passed across her visage, unseen and unseeable, but undeniably present. "No!" Travis snapped, swatting at the shadowy villain, but it was gone before he could throttle it in his palm. He grunted loudly at his failure.

"What?" Gavin whisper-called from the other side of the room.

"Why are you whispering?" The disapproval in Kaylyn's expression was evident in her voice.

"It just…I don't know…it felt appropriate."

Travis shook his head. "It was…nothing. But I need some light."

Gavin raised his phone, happy to oblige, but Kaylyn shot him down. "What for?"

"I just need to *see!*" Travis was frustrated as much as he was concerned. No further vision had passed across Alyssa's face but, somehow, he felt that it was still present in the room. Waiting for him to let his guard down.

"Not good enough," Kaylyn proclaimed. "No wasting the lights unless it's absolutely necessary."

"I think we could all do with a little light, though," Malachi chimed in. "Just for a few minutes, for some comfort."

"No. Absolutely not."

"Listen to Kaylyn, guys," Dorian prodded. "Who knows how much power we're going to need to use before morning."

They fell into disgruntled silence, Malachi pouting and Travis stroking Alyssa's hair while tensing so hard that his shoulder threatened to separate.

"Oh!" After a few minutes, Malachi finally broke the silence with an unexpectedly upbeat exclamation. "You know what, I think there *are* lights. I'm pretty sure—earlier, after Brady died—I ran into the basement, and I'm pretty sure that I saw some cans of kerosene and, possibly, some lamps. Then we wouldn't have to worry about our phone batteries for a while. Would that be okay?" He inquired of Kaylyn, not entirely sure as to why he needed her permission, but also knowing that he would get nowhere without it.

Even in chaos she still seemed to be the one with the most control over the plans.

Not one to wait for a go-ahead, Travis announced, "Yeah, I'll get them," but he didn't move.

Finally, Alyssa said, "You can't go alone."

"Wasn't planning on it, thanks."

The room went quiet, no one wanting to commit to leaving the safety of the space, even if it was for the long-term good. With a deep sigh, Malachi offered, "Okay. I'll go with you."

"We all go, or no one goes," Gavin intoned, and no one fought him, although the initial lack of motion suggested that the 'no one goes' option was in most favour around the circle.

But when Travis shifted up, Alyssa immediately followed suit, and then the rest were standing and ready. "Don't touch me," Kaylyn whispered to Dorian, shaking his hand away. Realizing that everyone had heard the momentary lovers' quarrel, she tempered her words. "I just feel safer if I'm free to run, right now."

By contrast, Travis gripped Alyssa's hand tightly as they pressed through the open door and back to the living room. When out of earshot of the rest, he whispered quietly in her ear, "I'll never let go."

As they trekked past the kitchen, Irina cried out to them—or, continued crying out to them—now, in a more directed screech. "You are pigs! You are scum! You are the reason this is happening. God will rid the world of the base and low!"

Malachi almost turned back, made a run for her ropes but, although he could not see who strode behind him, he could feel the presences of Travis, Alyssa, and Gavin, hear their footfalls. An impediment to hope.

Kaylyn lit her phone light as she held the door open for the rest. "Make it quick. I'm at one percent."

They shuffled past her into the garage with renewed vigour. Without Kaylyn, only Gavin's phone remained an option, and he'd only had time to half-charge it before the power had gone out that afternoon.

Travis pressed to the front of the group, feeling around in the shadows as Kaylyn's light left only part of the room dimly illuminated.

"I think it's somewhere in this area?" Malachi said from a few feet away. In the darkness, they spread about, losing the sensation of their bodies next to each other. Travis wrapped his arm around Alyssa's waist as they ducked down, scraped along the floor.

"Ow!" Mallory cried out as she spiked her finger on an unseen tool.

"Careful," Kaylyn commanded from the stairs, where she tried to use her leverage to share her light around the room below, creating shadows and generally being of little aid.

"Thanks," Mallory muttered, before slapping a hand hard over her mouth. How dare she direct sarcasm at Kaylyn!

From behind, someone knocked her leg. "Watch out, please."

No one replied.

"What did they look like?" Gavin called out.

"Um, I don't know…" Malachi started. "Kerosene lamps?" He hummed in nervous thought, trying desperately to find a description. "Roundish and glass with handles at the top? I'm pretty sure they're on this side…"

The room echoed with the violent clatter of objects of various sizes and weights smacking to the ground. Just when it seemed that the sound had stopped, more came. A repetitive beat of destruction.

"Is everyone okay?" Dorian called out, his footsteps striding back and forth across the room before disappearing into silence with the rest of their unlit bodies.

They all listened, waiting. And, after a moment of quiet, Malachi groaned. Lowly at first, but soon at growling pitches.

"What happened," Travis asked as Gavin and Mallory approached from the other side of the room, feeling slowly with their toes in the darkness.

"I'm fine," Malachi said, though he didn't sound fine. "Just knocked some things off of the shelf."

Kaylyn whipped her light over to where the bulk of the group was, but it had gone dim and, a moment later, they were cast into complete darkness. "Gavin, get your phone out," Kaylyn commanded, as he fumbled with his pocket messily, dropping the phone to the floor.

"Good job, Gav."

"Are you hurt?" Alyssa pressed of Malachi.

"I don't think…wait, I'm wet. Is this blood? Am I covered in blood? Oh my God, I think I'm covered in blood."

"Is it yours?" Travis asked.

"It…I don't know…it…"

Gavin's finger knocked his phone a few feet away and he followed the scrape along the floor until his hand clasped around it.

"I don't know whose." Malachi sniffed deeply. "It—it smells like something. It smells like…gas."

Gavin mashed at his screen but it had cracked in the fall, leaving spider lines overtop the flashlight button. He pressed, turned the screen, had to type in his passcode through further breaks and dents.

Something clicked airily from behind Malachi.

Gavin yanked down the menu and finally threw the light upon the group.

But no—the light app hadn't worked and his finger was still mashing futilely. So, why had the room suddenly become bright? And hot?

He lifted his head, along with the others, to witness the spectacle of Malachi going up in flames.

24. Revelation

THE GAS HELPED the flame travel quickly, engulfing his entire body as he screamed and swore, cried out in violent pain. But the crackling sound of the fire ate away even more loudly at his voice. The rest of the group instinctively stepped back from the danger, struggling to process what they could possibly do to save him.

"I'll get water!" Alyssa cried, turning and racing for a sink, now visible at the edge of the room, but Travis lunged out to grab her.

"It's a gas fire! You're only going to make it worse!"

"Blankets!" Gavin exclaimed, guiding Mallory up the stairs, where they grabbed Kaylyn, one by each arm, and dragged her with them to the bedrooms.

Travis led the charge about the basement in search of anything that might help, Alyssa and Dorian following his example. "There's gotta be sand or something around in a place like this!" he cried out over Malachi's screams. "There's gotta be…"

But as he turned to face the others, he found the light glowing brighter around him. Malachi had started to run, trying desperately to blow the fire away with the wind he created.

"Don't!" Travis screamed as the flames snaked higher and wilder.

But Malachi had no ability to process the world around him anymore, or perhaps no ears left to hear the command.

Travis dove to the ground as Malachi raced past, barely avoiding being incinerated. He leapt back up just as Gavin, Mallory, and Kaylyn returned with handfuls of crumpled up bedsheets and blankets.

"Throw them down!" Travis commanded, racing to the bottom of the stairs. He caught as many of them as he could as they fluttered open in the fall and nearly sent him slipping to the floor.

"Come on." He tossed a few ends to Alyssa, now approaching from the opposite side of the room.

Malachi made a wild turn toward the garage door, though he surely did not know he had done so.

"Go!" Travis cried out, as the pair of them charged with their bedsheets, throwing them atop Malachi as he sputtered to remove the impediments. They returned to the other side of the room to grab more as Gavin rushed his own set of sheets down the stairs to join the effort.

Another. Another. Until, finally, Malachi was crumpled on the ground under a world's weight of sheets.

The darkness they were cast back into didn't last for long, as Dorian came up with a kerosene lamp, properly lit, revealing a collection of others ready by its side. "Is he…?" Dorian began.

With a glance back at the rest of the room, Travis took the first step forward and began tossing blankets aside. As he moved the cloth, the room became progressively more aware of the pungent aroma wafting through the air. The fire, the smoke, the burnt meat.

Mallory gagged but held her stomach, if barely.

"Go faster," Kaylyn demanded, stepping forward to help with the reveal and tossing away sheets, wildly.

As they reached the bottom and pulled away the last blanket, everyone took a step back.

Malachi lay, black and charred, no longer burning, but no longer burning with life, either. Needing to be sure, Travis stepped forward and tentatively laid a hand upon Malachi's neck, searching for a pulse. He recoiled quickly, looking down at burnt fingers.

"Just check if he's breathing," Alyssa suggested, and Travis dropped down to watch Malachi's chest, or what was left of it, shirt largely burnt away and his torso showing holes of burnt-out flesh.

Travis shook his head, trembling at the intense heat that wafted into his face, his eyes. "He's gone."

"I think we've found the culprit," Dorian mused from the other side of the room, where the tragedy had begun. He bent down and came back up with a used match held lightly between his thumb and forefinger. "This wasn't an accident."

"Did any of us actually think it was?" Travis let the words fall hard as they all stared at each other, knowing they should have been running from the scene, from the smell, but all so inured to the inevitable death that the prospect of running didn't offer the comfort that it once did. After a few moments of grim contemplation, Dorian flicked the match to the floor.

"Come on, let's get out of here." He bent to light a few more lamps as the rest headed for the stairs, Gavin and Mallory hanging behind to help carry the lights up to the rest.

They deposited the lamps on the living room table, finally having the chance to look upon each other's faces, once more, taking in the lines and bags that had formed over the course of the day, the dishevelled hair, the ripped clothing. The blood on Alyssa's shin from where she'd smashed it into the stairs had seeped through her pants, though she could no longer feel it. Gavin, Kaylyn, and Mallory's clothes still stuck to them from the hours in torrential downpours. Travis still had blood on his collar, though he had washed Brady's blood completely from his hair.

"Well, I think we know what we have to do." Gavin broke the silence, glancing past the rest of the group to the shadows in the kitchen.

"No," Kaylyn cut in, before he'd even had a chance to speak his mind.

"She's innocent," Gavin declared. "We know that, now. Irina can't have done this." Gavin started toward the kitchen and Kaylyn grabbed his wrist.

"We don't know for sure."

"She was tied up, Kaylyn," Travis reasoned. "We kinda do."

"She could've had help."

"From who? She's the only one who had means and motive, remember? That's the only reason we voted to tie her up in the first place. She doesn't have means anymore."

Kaylyn opened her mouth to respond but came up with nothing. Dorian put a consoling hand on her shoulder as they followed the rest of the group to the kitchen.

"What happened? What have you done?" Irina spat as they approached. "Where is my boyfriend?"

Gavin grimaced as he looked to the rest of the group, but none dared to deliver the news. With a breath, he went straight for the simplest route: "Malachi's dead."

Irina took a moment to process, before crying out, "NO! You have done this. It cannot be true! Why do you lie?"

With a hard swallow, Gavin ignored her words, her yanks at her chains, as he struggled to find the knots and undo the ropes. No one else would get close.

It took several minutes to loosen the knots and to let the bonds thud to the floor. But, when she was finally free, Irina wasted no time. "This is your fault!" She lunged at Kaylyn, knocking her out of Dorian's hands and wrestling her to the ground. "If you had not done this—if you had not spread your lies—I would have been there to protect my boyfriend! I would have been there to protect him from you!" She struck Kaylyn's face, hard, with an open palm, twice, three times, before Kaylyn managed to shove her attacker upward.

This did little but inspire further rage, and Irina came down from her new point of leverage to deliver a powerful fist to Kaylyn's chin. Kaylyn cried out and closed her eyes, now batting wildly with her hands until one connected with Irina's neck and sent her backward, falling over her knees and onto her back. Kaylyn was quick to her knees and pounced upon Irina, aiming for the eyes. And she might have made contact if Dorian hadn't intervened, grabbing her around the shoulders and trying to drag her away from Irina.

His protection was short-lived, however, as Irina now had time to bound to her feet and chase Kaylyn down, blocked out by Dorian, but close enough to deliver a resounding headbutt to Kaylyn's lip. Alyssa cringed. Kaylyn bled.

Travis flinched, as if to help, but Alyssa held him tightly and he stayed, safe, with her. With a look to them, Gavin shook, hyperventilated, tried to shake off the stress but all he could manage was a whimper. He entered the fray unwillingly, but necessarily, trying to soothe Irina as he took a blow to the eye. Gavin dropped to a knee for a moment before rising again and taking another unintentional shot to the head, this time from Kaylyn attempting to reach past his shoulder.

Though he was weak, he pressed on with all his might, separating Irina from Kaylyn and guiding her to the edge of the island, while Dorian took Kaylyn to the wall and pressed her up against it, looking deeply into her eyes and trying to calm her with his gaze.

"Just stop, just stop, please," Gavin cried as Irina struggled, flailed, spat Russian curses in his face.

Travis patted Alyssa's hand lightly before letting go and striding over to help, the majority of the worst of it now passed. He laid a hand on Irina's shoulder and advised, "Just let it go. There's no good in fighting each other."

"This is on her. She is the one you should be stopping!"

"Okay, okay," Travis soothed. "You're right. It's her fault. But there's nothing we can do about that now. Let's just move forward. Can we let go? Will you do anything if Gavin lets go?"

She glared at him with falcon eyes before blinking in disgust and letting the tension fall from her shoulders. "You can let go."

Cautiously, Gavin released his hold and Irina's posture crumpled down a few inches. She took two deep breaths. Then charged at Kaylyn.

In kind, Kaylyn clawed at Dorian, trying to get away.

But Travis' quick reflex to swipe Irina's legs away with his ankle ended the war before it could recommence. Arms outstretched, Irina fell, spreadeagled, to the ground, her chin taking the brunt of the fall and the clatter of her teeth making even Kaylyn wince, before she smiled triumphantly at her win.

Awkwardly, Gavin approached Irina from behind and, not sure of what else he could do, placed a tentative knee upon her back, looking to the others for further instruction. But the others had more pressing matters to attend to.

"We need to get back into a safe space," Travis noted. "Back to the bedroom is an option."

"I don't like the window being there…" Alyssa walked to Travis and wrapped herself around his arm.

"We need a secondary escape, somewhere."

"Can't we all just be ready to attack if someone tries coming in the door?"

"Maybe we could…" But they would never discover what they could do. Gavin had barely started speaking before Irina took her opportunity. With his head turned upward, she bucked her back, sending him toppling floorward while she drove a shoulder into Dorian and knocked him away.

"I'll kill you!"

"Good luck," Kaylyn retorted with a shoulder to Irina's already sensitive teeth.

Dorian tried to grab them both as Gavin struggled up, pain searing through his back. Alyssa ventured forward, not sure what to do, but knowing she needed to get involved. She pitched over Gavin's outstretched leg and entered the fight on an unintended run, barely avoiding an elbow to the neck.

Unable to keep his head from spinning whilst upright, Gavin drove for an ankle—whose ankle, he could not be sure—and dragged back.

"Hey!" Alyssa cried out. "That's me!" He released and was promptly kicked in the face by another unidentifiable party. The five of them sputtered in an awkward dance of fists and bones, blood and teeth. Kaylyn kept one eye closed from a hard strike; Irina flinched every time she moved her head and pain shot through her entire face.

"Guys!" Travis called, but none of them cared.

"GUYS!" They continued, but something gave them pause. Another slap from Irina to Kaylyn's cheek ended the battle, as Kaylyn gave no response, looking back at Travis. Dorian froze, Alyssa gasped, and Gavin rose to his feet, dizzy, but lucid.

Across the island, Travis knelt on the floor. At first, it looked as though he was strangling Mallory, his hands pressed hard around her neck. But the fresh blood upon his shirt and hands, bleeding through his fingertips, showed that, no matter how much pressure he applied, he would not be able to save her.

He moved aside and sat on the floor in a defeated posture, looking down upon the jagged, messy slit across Mallory's neck.

25. Division

"SO, WE SPLIT up." Dorian sighed. "After all that, I think it's the only way."

"A-alone?" Alyssa shuddered, eyes flickering to the staircase and whatever demons lay in the basement.

"No," Dorian calmed her. "No, of course not alone. But in smaller groups." He bit his lip. "I think it's pretty obvious, at this point, that these two can't be in the same room as each other without a murder occurring, and we've had enough of that, as it is." All eyes flashed back to Mallory in an acknowledgement of respect. None had time or energy to cry, anymore. And their hearts were beating too fast to let them focus on much else but the pressure in their chests.

"Two groups of three," Travis offered from his spot on the floor. He hadn't moved in several minutes.

"What does it matter?" Gavin managed through heavy breaths. "This thing is picking us off even when we're all together. Groups, alone. There's nothing we can do at this point."

"Stop talking like that," Kaylyn snapped. "When was the last time any of us noticed Mallory?"

A few glances were exchanged. "When we first came up from the basement," Travis suggested.

"Anyone any later?" Kaylyn raised her eyebrows, pushing away from Dorian, who made sure to stay between her and Irina.

"I don't think so," Alyssa said.

"So, we don't know when this happened or who did it. It could've been any of us. Or anyone else in the house."

"Except me," Irina shot. Everyone ignored her.

"DJ said he'd go into town when the storm stopped, and it's getting close now." They glanced to the window and agreed that the rain was slowing. It had been a while since thunder had crashed through the walls.

"Not that going into town will help much," Dorian reminded them.

"But who knows what connections he may have after all this time. He probably knows where the police live and he can go get them. We just need to hold out until then."

"So, until then, we stay in two rooms." Travis ran a bloody hand through his hair, barely noticing the sticky streaks, anymore. "Me, Alyssa, and Irina in one; Kaylyn, Dorian, and Gavin in the other."

Gavin grunted.

"You got a problem with that?" Travis asked with slight frustration.

"No." Gavin leaned against the counter, head resting on his arms. "I just can't believe that's all that's left of us."

"Right." Travis pulled himself up to face the group. "Which room do you want?" He looked to Dorian.

"There was one that was supposed to have a lock on it, wasn't there?" Gavin cut in.

Kaylyn went through her mental list from the previous night. "Irina and Malachi's room."

"We stay there," Irina insisted.

"And let you have a geographical advantage? I don't think so."

"Geographical advantage." She spat on the ground. "To do what?"

"To kill."

"You see that I am the one person who cannot have been killing and, still, you think I kill."

"Let's just stay away from anyone staying in their own room." Travis rubbed the bridge of his nose, exasperatedly. "Just in case. So, the three of you stay there, and the three of us will take Kaylyn and Dorian's room."

"That's fair," Dorian agreed. Kaylyn and Irina both made to protest, but having little reason to do so aside from the fight, both backed down quickly.

"All right." Travis led the way. "Let's go."

*

"I THINK YOU can put that down, now," Kaylyn groaned at Gavin, who held a high heel in one hand and a battery-operated, handheld vacuum in the other. He'd insisted that Dorian take him to the boiler room before settling into Irina and Malachi's room, where Dorian had recalled seeing the cleaning equipment. "It's been three hours and no one's come through that door."

"Besides, what're you going to do anyway?" Dorian smirked slightly. "Suck them up?"

"Who knows how ghost matter works."

"Oh, my God, Gavin. This isn't a ghost." Kaylyn rolled her eyes.

"Well, your number one theory is out the window, so it's time we give mine a try."

"Just put the stuff down," Dorian advised, more peaceably this time. "Your arms are going to be tired by the time they come to the door, anyway."

Grimacing at the truth of the matter, but not wanting to admit defeat, Gavin placed the objects at his sides without a word, but continued to stand by the door, ready to pounce.

*

"YOU SICKEN ME." Irina broke a long and very pleasant silence—as pleasant as it could get under the circumstances.

Travis, arm wrapped around Alyssa, one hand on her knee while she nuzzled her face into his neck, on a rare, bloodless patch, raised an eyebrow, unimpressed. "Just because you're heartless doesn't mean the rest of us have to be."

"Travis, be nice." Alyssa stroked his leg.

"You know what I do not understand?" Irina lounged back on the shag rug, leaning against the wall. "Why would you"—she gestured to Alyssa—"great beauty, many options, much money—settle for *him*, destitute farm boy."

"My family doesn't work on a farm," Travis grumbled, though he refused to offer reality in return, which was that his father was a perpetually

unemployed alcoholic and his mother sold low quality
bags produced by a sketchy company.

"He cares. He cares and loves and does everything for me. I love him." Alyssa was defensive. "And
Malachi was the same for you."

"Malachi was convenience. I am allowed to stay
in country. He gives me that; I give him this." She
gestured to her perfect figure, her long legs, her glis-
tening, pale skin.

"That's what's sickening." Alyssa shook her head
and turned away, refusing to look at Irina any longer.

Travis smirked, impressed at the unexpected outburst. There was nothing more that needed to be said.

They sat in silence for a while longer before Irina
felt the need to disrupt the peace, once again. "I need
to use restroom."

"Then go." Travis gestured dismissively toward
the door.

"I will not go alone." She crossed her arms.

"It's just down the hall, come on."

"No, someone must wait for me."

Alyssa and Travis looked to each other, neither
wanting to be alone with her and neither wanting to
be alone.

"If no one comes, I pee here."

And, though she probably didn't mean it, that
got both of them up quickly. "Okay." Travis grimaced. "We go as a group."

"Ha!" Irina chortled. "You think I let man hear
me use restroom? Sit down, silly boy."

"I'm not staying here alone."

"Yet, you think I should go out there all by myself. You are an inconsistent one."

"Okay." Alyssa held her head in frustration.
"First, we walk Travis downstairs to the other room
so he can be with the others; then, I'll take you to the
bathroom."

"This is too long of a walk. It is right here."

"Do you want company or not?" Alyssa snapped,
almost shocking herself.

Irina gave her falcon glare, but it had no effect,
anymore. Not after a night of greater terrors. "Fine."

Even carrying their kerosene lamps, the house
was dark, and the shadows cast by the dim light were
almost worse than seeing nothing at all. They
clumped together, too close for Travis' comfort, as Irina's rear continually bumped into his groin. And,
they were halfway down the steps before he started to
wonder whether she was doing it exclusively to
bother Alyssa. After all, their bodies were amongst
the few things clearly visible in the dying light.

If it bothered her, though, Alyssa said nothing.
They reached the door to Irina and Malachi's bedroom without a word or incident. Travis knocked
slowly. "Hey, it's us." No response. He tried the door
handle, locked. "Guys, let us in."

The door flung open and Gavin leapt out, violently throwing a shoe in their direction while sucking
wildly with a vacuum cleaner. Travis, Alyssa, and Irina
jumped back as Gavin shut the power off and slapped
a hand over his heart.

"Can never be too careful," he said sheepishly as
Travis entered the room.

"Alyssa's taking Irina to the bathroom, so I'm hanging out here for a while. They'll come back to get me when they're done. So, Gavin—try not to suck them to death when that happens?"

Gavin shut the door and Alyssa and Irina just heard him say, as they walked away, "If you'd been a ghost, I would've been a hero."

"Come on," Alyssa prodded, entering the restroom and dropping her kerosene lamp on the counter. "Let's get this over with."

Irina followed, stood in front of Alyssa, looking her up and down, then scoffed. "You don't think I let you in restroom with me while I do private business?"

Alyssa spread her arms widely, exasperated. "You just said you wouldn't come alone."

"I said I do not come alone, but I did not say I would let you in restroom with me. Out."

"No. If I'm waiting out there, we're going back to get Travis, first."

"I said already, I do not let a man hear me do my business." She shook her head. "You are woman. You should understand."

"What's wrong with you?"

"Get out. Now." She did not scream, but the command was absolute.

"No. You're going to suck it up and *'do your business'* with me in the room, sis. Whether you like it or not."

Irina stood quietly for a moment, eyeing Alyssa up. Then she took the other woman's shoulders and pressed her from the room. Alyssa dug in her heels, but between the surprise attack and a defined strength difference, she was overmatched. She was still stumbling back from Irina's push when she saw the Russian slam the door in her face and lock it quickly.

"I will be not two minutes," Irina called from within.

No. No, that was two minutes too many. Alyssa beat against the door. "Let me in! Let me in!"

She looked around in the dark, her lamp still on the counter in the bathroom. "Please," she cried. "Don't leave me out here." She felt a presence from behind, the one that had grabbed her ankle and sent her sputtering to the ground earlier.

She whipped around, looking for a sign of it, but saw nothing. In the tiny crack of light from under the bathroom door, she could see little more than black and shadow. But she knew something was there. She could feel it. It was reaching for her neck.

Something flickered across her vision.

She could not scream.

26. Gone

IRINA TOOK HER time washing her hands, cleaning the grime of the entire day out of her false fingernails. She was midway through the second round of soap when she heard a brush outside the bathroom door, and Alyssa stopped crying out to be let inside. *Petty bitch*, Irina thought, going in for a third wash.

She made sure that her hands were completely dry and sought around for moisturizer that was, tragically, absent, before finally sighing and heading for the door. She opened it quickly, irritably, staring daggers out into the basement. "Impatient..." she began, before looking about and discovering that no one was present to hear. "Predictable." She rolled her eyes. "Run on back to the boyfriend, you pathetic, useless..." She grabbed both kerosene lamps grumpily and returned to the bedroom, upstairs.

"You know, you are lucky that I made it back alive..." she began, ready to chide the girl for running, but found the room as empty as they'd left it.

A chill burrowed up her spine as she stood alone in the house, and she couldn't say for sure whether it was caused by the walls, the ghost, or her mind. Swallowing hard, but too proud to panic, even in front of no one but herself, she turned rigidly and headed back into the living room.

"Stop," she whispered to herself as her right hand began to shake. "Stop that at once!" She turned her cold eyes about the room and absorbed the nothingness. No one lurked in the shadows—she made sure to check. The rain had stopped outside, now, leaving only the cold chill of night behind, closing in upon The Little Maple Cabin on Spruce Road.

The kitchen was empty. She considered taking a knife from the block but had no interest in being falsely accused, once more. Still, the knife block caught her eye, and she couldn't help but notice that two knives were gone. One, the paring knife, she had taken. But the peeling knife…she was certain it had been there when she'd taken her weapon.

Feeling as though she was being watched, she whipped around quickly, but found the room empty. She returned downstairs as the thought suddenly struck her: what if they don't let me back in? After all, they would have let Alyssa or Travis back in in a heartbeat—they were friends—but with neither of them to vouch for her, she was the outsider amongst the group.

She may have been a manager and out of the social loop, but she knew the connections. Travis and Gavin had become fast friends when they started at the same time. Kaylyn, the party planner, had been an obvious add to their group-within-the-larger-group. Alyssa and Dorian may have been little more than significant others, despite having worked at The Palace, themselves, but they were tightly knit to the bunch as a result of their positions.

And then, there was Irina. An inconvenient add-on to the weekend, a tolerated friend-of-a-friend. Suddenly, she wished she'd endeared herself to them more.

But no—that was the fear talking. She couldn't get down on herself when she'd done nothing wrong and had had to deal with the frustrating antics of children for most of their acquaintance.

She reached the bottom of the steps and glanced about the basement, the pseudointellectual motivational posters. The couches that…no, no one was sitting on them. It was a trick of the light, or lack thereof. But her heart still beat aggressively at the thought.

Irina slipped past the bathroom and back to her former bedroom, knocking loudly on the door. "Let me in."

Travis answered with a hard expression, stepping out to follow, grudgingly, back to their room.

He stopped once in the main area, turning once about.

"Where is the other?" Irina asked as aloofly as possible, though she was now struck with the realization that she didn't want to admit.

"What are you talking about?" Even in the dim light, it was clear that Travis had gone ghostly pale.

"Where is…?" Irina began, but she couldn't bring herself to throw the blame about any longer.

"Weren't you with her? The entire time?" Travis' brain was still processing, not understanding as he looked in circles.

Gavin, Kaylyn, and Dorian made their way to the doorframe. "Where's Alyssa?" Gavin's eyes widened.

"It was not my fault that she could not stand alone for a minute…" Irina crossed her arms.

"You left her alone?" Travis did not wait for a response. He lunged at Irina and knocked her hard to the ground.

"You dare hit a woman?" she asked with indignance that even she, now, was struggling to pull off.

"Oh, I'm gonna do a hell of a lot more than that," he cried, wrapping his hands around her neck.

Eyes widening, Irina felt the pressure on her throat and, in contrast to the fight she'd shared with Kaylyn, where silent understanding left both knowing that the fight would end in little more than cuts and bruises, in this confrontation, she felt certain that he meant to kill.

She sucked in air as fast as she could before he applied the brunt of the pressure. He kept pressing. Arms useless in their slaps and strikes against the face and body of a man who had lost all feeling, she resorted to the nuclear option and brought her knee up into Travis' groin. But the man was a machine in those moments, feeling nothing, never moving his fingers from her throat.

"Travis, stop." Gavin raced behind his friend and tried to pull him off. "Don't do this!" Travis did not stop. But the moment of pull from Gavin was enough to afford Irina another quick breath before the pressure returned.

"Okay, okay." Dorian joined in, taking Travis by the shoulders and ignoring the searing pain as the incensed man bit down upon his forearm. "Just let her go."

"Don't let her go." Kaylyn glowered from the doorframe, watching it happen. "Finish the job, Travis."

But between Dorian and Gavin—or, at least, due to Dorian—Travis found himself yanked away and held back.

"Where did she go?" he cried. "Where did you put her?"

Irina choked, gagged, looked up for support but found only Kaylyn, weighing the thought of stomping down on the back of her neck. She pushed back and fought her way up, still gasping, still ailing. "She…just…disappeared…"

"Where?" Travis turned his attention to the more important matter. "Where did she go? When did you see her last?"

Irina tried to catch her breath, but this was taking much too long. Travis lurched past Dorian but was grabbed again before he could get all the way to Irina. "WHERE?"

"There." Irina coughed, pointing to the bathroom door, just a few steps away. "That…is where…I saw…her last…"

Travis broke in the direction of the bathroom, Dorian and Gavin not holding him back, anymore. "She must be around here?" He threw back the bath curtains in darkness, his lamp—dropped as he'd lunged for Irina's neck—still lying on the main room floor. Gavin recovered it and brought it in for light. Travis took almost no notice, grabbing it on the way by and flying into Mick and Brady's room.

He threw the sheets from the bed, leaving Mick's remains open to the air; flew under the beds; booted Mick's covered head across the room; then took the rest of the basement like a tornado.

"Help me look!" he demanded. "She has to be here, somewhere!"

They opened doors, threw belongings all over the floor, broke the television, kicked at drawers. But, mostly, it was Travis who did the damage, not caring whom he bumped into or what he destroyed in the mad dash for Alyssa.

"I looked upstairs," Irina managed as Travis headed in that direction. Instead, he changed course for the boiler room. They followed when they heard a vicious clatter, but discovered, only, that Travis had tossed the cleaning equipment aside in his recklessness.

"Go!" he cried. "Get out! Be useful!" And none of them begrudged him the criticism. They returned to looking under couches, behind dark shadows. And, shortly, Travis re-emerged, eyes manic, as he shot for the locked door.

"It's the only place she can be. It's the only place she can be," he kept repeating to himself, over and over. When pulling and kicking and smashing at the doorframe did nothing but hurt Travis' hands, he resorted to brute force, taking a few steps back and running at the door, not caring that the door didn't seem even to bend or acknowledge his pressure. He ran again, and again, his shoulder cracking with ever more painful crunches upon each instance of contact.

"HELP!" he cried out, and Gavin jumped to his aid, running into the door as well. But all for nothing, as it would not budge.

Travis cried, hot tears pouring down his face, as he beat upon the door with a bruised fist, softer and softer as the energy drained from his body, unable to break through the impenetrable wood.

"Tools," he managed weakly. "From the garage. Get me tools." Gavin took a few steps and found no one following.

"Come on, let's get him tools."

Kaylyn approached with a furtive whisper. "Do you really think there's a point? She can't possibly be back there."

"Where else?"

"Maybe the garage, or outside. Who knows where this guy took her?"

"This *thing*," Gavin corrected, and she wasn't in the mood to argue.

"Whatever, none of us have been able to get through that door, though. You think Alyssa suddenly found a way at the most inconvenient possible time."

"Isn't it worth trying?"

"At this point"—Kaylyn glanced back over her shoulder to see Travis weeping into the floor, banging his head against the door—"I don't think we should be moving around, anywhere, unless it's an emergency."

From above, a screech sounded through the dead night air, distant but unfamiliar, and definitely not human. All ears perked up, looking to the ceiling as though they would be able to see through to whatever atrocity was taking place beyond their world. The episode concluded with a violent, crunching crash. And that was when the entire foundation of the house began to shake.

27. Crash

GAVIN AND KAYLYN were the first to the stairs, with Irina close behind. Dorian reached for Travis, but Travis brushed him off, pushing away and racing for the steps.

"What was that?" Gavin cried as he rounded back toward the front door.

"Death," came Irina's ominous response as she shoved past Kaylyn, who tripped on the last step. There was no time to go back for her as Gavin and Irina raced to the front door and threw it wide to look out upon the wet night.

The ground was no longer shaking, but a new sound had joined the generally silent mix. It was as if something was sizzling from the side of the house, near the garage.

Gavin was hesitant to move past the doorstep alone, but wouldn't have to be first, as Irina pushed by in search of the disturbance. It did not take long to find.

The side of the house was cracked and broken, bricks falling away and metal bent and angular. Embedded into the side of the wall was a red sedan or, at least, what remained of one, as it had been crushed, largely beyond recognition, by impact with the wall. It was an old car, one that looked like it could barely survive the road. And, though it was dark in the vacuum of the night, the world barely illuminated by the single streetlight that was much too far away to expose any details, it was impossible not to notice the angry cloud of smoke billowing up from the car's engine, just beneath the rubble of the wall.

Irina continued to run toward the site as Gavin hesitated. "Wait, is it safe to get close?" But that was a stupid question, he realized. Because, of course, it wasn't safe.

He rushed forward to join her, slipping on the slick ground and faceplanting into the dirt driveway. His entire body covered in mud. Specks of stones and splintered twigs threatening to cut into the corners of his eyes. He jumped back up, trying to ignore the pain, but limping, now, half his body searing with each pounding step.

"What happened?" he called out, spitting bitter soil back to the ground. He peeled around to the driver's side window, where Irina now stood with a large, jagged rock in her right hand. "What are you doing?!"

She drove the rock hard into the window once, twice. He just got there in time to see the third smash break through the glass and shatter over the driver, not that he noticed much from his position, hunched over, his head down on the wheel and blood pouring from his left ear.

"DJ?" Gavin reached through the window, scarring his arm along the edge of the glass as he pressed for the man's back, trying to get his attention, to wake him from his unconsciousness. "DJ?"

The large man did not move. He remained in position, broken, looking half his usual size.

"Out of my way." Irina shoved Gavin aside and reached to DJ's neck, feeling for a pulse. She held her fingers there for several moments, waiting. "There is no point," she concluded.

She began to remove her fingers just as DJ shot around and wrapped his massive hand about her tiny wrist. His hollow eyes were deep and seemed to suck in all that the night had not already taken. Irina screamed out, her wrist crushed within his grasp. "Let go! Let me go!" But DJ only squeezed tighter, until Irina's hand started to turn cold. She tried to reach in with her other arm, to save herself, but the man took up so much space through the window that there was no means of getting anything in to save her.

"DJ," Gavin called out, trying to get through to what was clearly a dazed and broken mind. "DJ, listen to me. What happened? What *happened*?"

He wouldn't let go, but his grip stopped getting stronger. DJ's breathing increased and his eyes focussed, widely, on what he was doing. "Ah!" He threw Irina's wrist back, nearly tossing her to the ground in the process.

As he turned his head, Gavin saw the blood slicing down the other side of his face, as well, the shard of windshield glass stuck through his cheek, the bricks resting upon his knee.

"DJ," Gavin tried more softly, this time. "What happened?"

"I was…I was…" He looked around, glazed, as Gavin's eyes shot to the smoke still threatening them all from the front of the car. He quietly pleaded *Come on, come on.*

"I was going into town to…to…"

"To get the police?"

"Yes." His voice was becoming airy. He was slipping away. "The police. I wanted to get…but the roads…"

"They were winding?" Gavin continued to prod.

"No—I mean, yes—but no, they were…wet…slippery. I…lost control. The car—wouldn't stop…"

"You couldn't get control of the car?"

"No—no. The car…I couldn't…stop…"

"What do you mean?" Gavin's eyes flitted to the smoke, once more. They couldn't have had much time left. "Why would you want to stop? You were going into town, weren't you?"

"I was going into town, yes…" DJ's head started to drift back toward the headrest, a small, empty smile forming on his lips. "Going into town…"

"But why were you trying to stop? What did you want to do?"

"I couldn't stop. Couldn't stop the car. The brakes…the brakes were cut…"

His hollow, grey eyes rolled back, slowly, in his head until only the whites were left. His body went rigid and his mouth hung open wide. He was dead.

"We get out of here now," Irina commanded.

And, though he hated to leave the once-powerful man behind, Gavin only needed to look at how greatly the smoke had grown to know that there was no time to salvage his body. He stutter-stepped back, nearly slipping and instinctively grabbing out for Irina's shoulder for support.

"The brakes were cut," he mumbled in her ear as he stabilized. "The brakes were cut. There's no way out!"

She shoved him off and he turned his ankle, but managed to stay upright. Limping even more than before, he cried out with each step. They were halfway to the front door, Irina in the lead, when the car exploded in a supernova of light and heat. Gavin felt his back being burned as he leapt forward on instinct.

Irina, too, took to the ground, covering her head lest the carnage of the car fly in their direction. They were not sure for how long they lay and covered, their ears ringing from the boom. Finally, shakingly, Gavin rose again, feeling his body to make sure that all of him was there. "Is everyone all right?" he cried out, more loudly than necessary, but still hardly able to hear whether he was talking, at all.

Irina took to her feet, as well, trying to act as though she was not shaken, but her knees giving her away. Gavin scanned the night, looking for the others. But they were not there. "Where are they? Where's everyone else?"

Irina faced him, her countenance shadowed ominously in the flickering fire from her lamp. "They never came out."

Gavin wasn't sure whether the heat from the fire was simply wearing off, or if he'd suddenly gone cold, but this didn't feel right. "That's not like them. Why would they wait when we went out." He looked to the doorstep. "They're not even watching from the door."

He pushed forward, knocking past Irina, heart pounding through his chest. "Travis? Kaylyn? Dorian?" His foot caught and he pitched forward on the front porch, but he kept going as though nothing had happened, his kerosene lamp swinging wildly and threatening to light the wood on fire.

Gavin burst through the front door and turned in wild circles, shadows and emptiness creeping in upon him. He saw Mav, still bloodied in the corner; Mallory still lying in the hall.

Irina arrived behind him, standing upon the threshold, blocking him in with the devil, once again. "Where did they go?" He whipped around to face Irina before stepping forward with a low, sickly splash.

Gavin lowered the lamp and lifted his foot, hobbling on his injured ankle as he examined the thick, red mass that covered his sole.

To his left lay Kaylyn, eyes open and amazed shock etched across her face. And below her mouth, her neck still pumped the last of its blood from the jagged, messy slice across her throat.

28. Run

TRAVIS CRASHED DOWN the stairs and stumbled over the bottom steps, face striking the floor, but not slowing down as he broke from the figure approaching behind him. This was a mistake; he knew it was a mistake. There was no escape down here. And who knew what that sound was outside? What terrors it might have brought. Outside, he heard Gavin's distant voice fading into the vacuum of night as he slid further into the centre of the room.

There was nowhere to go in the open concept, nowhere to hide. Making it all the more maddening that he couldn't find Alyssa anywhere. He saw the figure at the top of the stairs, fading in his sight as he cut to the right and flew under the bed in Mick's room.

His best hope—his only hope—that he was hidden well enough to kill time, to make a plan. He could've gone into any room. Maybe the others would be searched first. Maybe he'd have a chance to burst out and head back upstairs, to disappear into the night, before he could be caught.

Kaylyn was dead. But he hadn't wanted her.

The strike to the back of Travis' head as he stood over the broken girl might have been enough to fell him if he hadn't turned at just the right moment and been ready for it. He'd fought, kicked, spat, and swiped. Had barely gotten away, although the slash across his Achilles threatened to be the final blow.

Now he breathed heavily as he watched the black flow past his vision, heading in his direction. No luck. Maybe he didn't deserve it.

Travis held his breath, trying to keep it in, but his heart beat so loudly that it threatened to press the air out of his lungs. In the dark, it was impossible to tell whether the figure was right in front of him, or on the other side of the room. But he was here. Travis could feel his presence searching, waiting…

Reaching underneath the bed and grabbing for his leg.

Travis started, smacking his head hard upon the bottom of the bed. This time, the blood in his hair was his own.

He swam along the hardwood, slipping on the faded lacquer, trying to claw his short fingernails between the boards as he was dragged back with a sharp, strong grip.

There was no way forward. His best bet was to let himself be taken and come prepared. Travis gripped hard to the leg of the bed, waiting as the pulling came harder and harder and, just when it reached its hardest point, he released and was flung out from within his sanctuary with such force as to toss the figure back, behind him.

For a moment, the thought of fighting flickered inside his brain, and that hesitation was a mistake. What advantage he'd gained from the surprise release was forgotten and the figure was atop him, again.

Travis bucked up, felt long fingers around his waist, but subdued his pursuer with a violent, high blow with his elbow. The grip loosened, just slightly, but enough that Travis was able to drive his way forward, through the darkness, and straight into the doorframe. With no forward movement available without being caught in the momentum of the one behind him, he curled around the wall, counting on the darkness and his socked feet to mask his path into the bathroom, where he stood just within the door, hoping that the other would not turn in that direction.

A few moments passed. A minute. But for how long would he be safe? He could scarcely make out the staircase, but the flickering glow of the kerosene lamp in the kitchen provided a general idea of where it might be.

In the middle of the room, he heard something fall. This was his chance.

He shot from his hiding spot and crashed straight into the staircase railing, taking the shot hard to the gut. Sputtering, and giving away his position, he fell back, but pressed forward, throwing himself up the stairs on all fours until he could manage his way up.

His pursuer was taking his time. He could feel it. Nothing behind him when there easily could have been. He burst into the dim shadows of the living room and curled to his left. From outside, he heard an explosion, but he didn't have time to go investigate.

He raced for the front door, the only escape.

But something stood before him, white and ethereal. Billowing in a windless vacuum and seeming to grow as he approached.

It faced away but turned to meet him.

The only light amongst the darkness, Mick's translucent form sucking all heat from a room that hadn't seemed to have any to begin with.

He held his severed, blindfolded head in his right hand. A bearded ball. Dark, bruisy patches interrupting the powdery white from where he'd been kicked, multiple times, across the room.

Slowly, the spectre raised its left hand in a firm, deliberate point toward the back door.

Travis had no time to think, to wonder how hard he'd really hit his head downstairs, to wonder whether to trust or to doubt. But the path to egress was blocked and he wasn't ready to test how solid the ghostly figure before him may have been.

He turned sharply on his heel, sliding along the floor for a few feet before grinding to a halt and accepting the ghost's directions as gospel.

He raced for the sliding doors, toward the deadly back patio, not knowing what he would find, not knowing if it would hold him. But it was his only chance now.

The figure had appeared a few feet behind him. He could feel the slow approach, the weight of death ready to strike down upon him at any moment.

Travis struggled with the latch, finally got it up, but still could not force the door open. He had seconds now, maybe less. Desperately, he kicked at the seal and, miraculously, it budged. He threw all of his weight into the handle. And found himself blocked by the screen.

There was no time to play with another lock.

Shoulder down, he drove through the torn wire mesh and vaulted over the hole that Malachi had left, not able to see it but estimating its position.

The cold air stung his face as he flew through the darkness, feet searching desperately for stable ground.

He made contact with the wood and felt relief crash through him as he brought his other heel down, hard.

And that was when the rotten wood collapsed beneath his weight. He grasped at the splinters and spikes but they, too, broke off and disintegrated beneath his touch. Next he knew, he was falling through the air, an unknowable, unseeable distance to the dark ground below. He cycled his arms; he screamed out into the emptiness. Nothing could break his fall but the cold, hard ground.

From above, the figure peered down into the chasm, observing the broken body below carefully to ensure that it could not get up. His legs were bent backward, his arms in crooked directions. Travis lay, a broken man, only his hair still flowing behind him in the dead of the night.

Satisfied, the figure nodded once to itself and pulled the door gently shut before returning to the house to wait. To wait for its final prey and to finish the job.

29. Conclusions

GAVIN DROPPED TO Kaylyn's side, but the effort was futile, as he was so used to it being. He just couldn't go forward without knowing for sure, without at least trying to do all that he could.

"Leave her. She did not matter, anyway." Irina spat next to Kaylyn's body. And she was lucky that it missed because, if it hadn't, Gavin would have been even less forgiving than he was.

He jumped to his feet and shoved Irina hard against the wall behind him, not caring that she was taller or meaner or, very possibly, stronger. Adrenaline carried him and he could no longer think about anything but his hatred for this woman. "I gave you," he growled, low, from a place he'd never gone before in his life, "every chance. *Every bloody chance* to be a decent human being. And *this* is what you do. Every time. Every time you have a chance to be good or decent or kind, you choose to be a wicked bitch. I was on your side—d'you know that? When Kaylyn first said she thought you might've done it, I said 'no way, not a chance'. Now? Now, I don't really care. I wish we'd just stabbed you through the neck while you were tied up and we had the chance.

"No," he thought better of it. "Through the eyes. Through those horrible, disgusting, bird eyes of yours that you think make you strong, make you better than the rest of us. But you're not. You're human and you die a human. And, I swear to God, if you take even one more step out of line, I don't care who does it, but I'll make sure, one way or another, that you go before I do, if just so I can watch the life drain out of your useless, bitch face."

Irina did not fight back. Maybe it was shock, maybe it was confusion, maybe—it wasn't regret— but fear? "I am sorry," she said, maybe the first time in her life that those words had come out of her mouth. And now Gavin didn't know what to do. So ready, he had been, to throw her to the ground and finish the job that Travis had started when she'd lost Alyssa.

Instead, he just let go, allowing her body to fall to the ground in front of him.

Instinct wanted to apologize, to take it all back. But, if for Kaylyn's sake alone, as she watched on from beyond the grave, he could bear to do nothing else but recommence his walk through the house, in search of the others, in prayers that they were, some-how, safe.

It took a few moments to realize what was strange about the kitchen as they approached: light. A small flicker came from the table, infinitesimal, yet warm and inviting. A false call. An *ignis fatuus* over the swamp of blood left behind by Brady and Mallory.

"Travis?" Gavin squeaked, couldn't quite call out. "Dorian?" His own throat held back his force, part of him wondering whether he really wanted to find them, at all. Irina followed closely, suddenly seeming to appreciate the need for company and protection.

At the door to the living room, Gavin turned to Irina and, differences seeming immaterial for just that

moment, whispered, "Do you have a weapon or anything?"

She looked down to her false nails, now chipped
and muddy, the best she had. Her eyes turned back to
Gavin's and she shook her head, slowly.

He licked at dry lips, heart catching in his airways.
Finally, he managed, "If it comes down to it, we hit
them with these," he raised his lamp. She nodded
once, curt, but effective.

With a deep breath, Gavin burst into the living
room, seeking around and ready for a surprise attack,
but none was forthcoming. In all, the room looked
the same as it had before they'd travelled downstairs.

They crept past the kitchen to the garage door.
Deciding that the surprise method was his best opportunity at survival, Gavin kicked the door in hard,
only to find the room as devoid of life as it had been
earlier in the evening.

With a sigh of relief, he turned, only to find himself face-to-point with a knife.

He backed slowly into the garage door, now shut
behind him, jaw quivering, regretting every cruel word
he'd spoken to Irina just a few minutes ago.

But, slowly, she lowered the blade to her side and
stood calmly before him.

"You—what? How did you…?"

"Relax, child." The word clearly connoted a
dearth of intelligence, rather than being an endearing
pet name. "I took it from the block, just now. Now
we have our weapon. I do not desire to use it upon
you."

He wanted to respond, but no words would come beyond a pointless whimper, so he sucked back all thought of the knife and focussed upon the principal task at hand. "The garage is clear."

"We check the bedrooms." They entered one at a time, Gavin kicking the door wide and Irina taking the first steps through, knife raised and ready to kill. Each time, Gavin would turn to face the entrance as Irina cleared the room, guarding against a surprise attack.

And, each time, nothing came.

"The upstairs is empty," Irina noted. "It is best we leave now."

"Travis and Dorian." Gavin shook his head.

"Are probably dead. Or escaped already. We look and we die."

The rest of Gavin trembled along with his head, now. She was probably right. He knew that, but he also knew that, if they were still alive, he would not be able to live with himself, knowing he'd left them behind. Travis, at least. He barely knew Dorian, but Travis was his friend. One of his best. The last one left.

"Can't do that to them."

"And if they are the killers?"

"This is not the work of a man." Gavin looked to her resolutely. But seeing the fear in her eyes, that which she had hidden for so long but could no longer keep to herself, he deflated into a compromise. "If we don't find them downstairs, we get out. As fast as we can."

Irina grimaced but nodded once.

They headed for the steps just as a deep cry came from the basement. The low scream that had hidden behind the locked door throughout the weekend. They stopped at the top step. "You are sure?" Irina breathed slowly.

Gavin simply pressed forward.

"We start with Travis' bedroom. Then mine," he instructed, leading them past the door, the wailing growing as they neared before trailing them into the rooms. Travis and Alyssa's room was clear. Gavin, Mallory, and Mav's room had been left untouched since last night.

One more time past the door, Gavin reminded himself. Just one more time.

But the moment they re-entered the main room, the awful cry ceased and left a quiet, ominous vacuum that was much worse than the company of sound.

As they crossed the main room, Gavin stopped to look at the locked door, to consider it. On instinct, he jiggled the handle once. Still nothing. He shook his head.

"Come on, we're almost there," he whispered to Irina.

But Irina was not looking at him. She was looking past him to the centre of the expansive room, where the couches rested in front of the smashed television and the motivational posters they'd long ignored.

Her eyes were focussed on the near couch, and Gavin turned to follow her gaze.

Because, sitting there, back to them, was a head, just peeking over the couch's back, body slouched down and out of view. The hair was blonde, short.

Dorian.

They'd walked right past him on the way down and hadn't noticed in the dim flicker of their insufficient light.

The body shifted.

Both Gavin and Irina took a step back, cornered away from the staircase, but ready to fight for their lives.

And then, Dorian rose, slowly, confidently, and turned about to face them. He wore an empty expression, his deep blue eyes shadowed like holes in the darkness. Without a word, he walked around the far side of the couch to face them, standing near to the wall, hands clasped together in front of himself.

Gavin broke the silence without meaning to, the question bursting from his mind and flowing from his mouth before he could stop it: "Where's Travis?"

Dorian took a slow, deep breath, continuing to face them. Then, he shook his head once and looked almost—*almost*—sympathetic. "He's gone."

"It was you," Irina stated, did not ask. "It was you all this time."

Dorian fought against a small upward crinkle at the right side of his lips, though he did his best to remain neutral. "More or less."

"What did you do to him?" Gavin shook, wanting to step forward but knowing that he was best advised to keep his distance.

"Nothing," Dorian said, almost convincingly. "He just…took a nasty fall. Through the porch. Quite bloody, as far as I could tell. And I'm sure limbs weren't meant to bend that way." Now, he couldn't keep the small, sick smile from cracking across his face.

"What is wrong with you?" Irina asked uselessly, rhetorically.

But Dorian wanted to answer. "Quite a lot, probably. Never could *quite* figure out what it was, though. I'm just *one of those guys*, who sees a problem and figures: I'll make that go away. Some say, 'oh no, you can't do it like that!' I say, 'why not?'" he shrugged, casually, like it was a simple enough explanation that would be easily accepted.

Instead, Gavin's eyes widened as his brows knitted together in disgust and confusion. "What problem could possibly have…"—he wanted to say *murdering your friends* but couldn't bring the words to his lips—"…could possibly have *this* as the easiest solution."

"Well." Dorian leaned against the back of the couch, a regular old Saturday chat in the works. "You were in the way, so I got rid of you, can't really get much simpler."

It was not lost upon them that 'you' seemed to include those still living. Gavin wasn't sure he wanted to know, but he also didn't want to die without knowing. "In the way of what?"

"Oh, that. You're going to think it's so stupid and petty."

"I can think of many words, in three languages, but none comes close to 'stupid' nor 'petty'." Irina's fire was beginning to return the longer this conversation continued, and Gavin couldn't determine whether this was good or very, very bad.

"Well, long story short, I'm not who I say I am. In some ways, I guess I'm not really anyone." Dorian tilted his head side-to-side, thinking things through. "See, never really liked the family, poor forgotten child and all that jazz. Anyway, decided to take off one day with all the cash from the safe. *That* didn't go over well, and I had the police on my trail for a bit, blah-blah-blah. Hit someone with my car, figured, I'm in this far, might as well make the most of it. Sold the organs on the black market because, what the hell? Doctor I worked with was a bit of a stickler for little things like 'getting paid', you know. So, I offed him, too.

"Pretty sure there are warrants out for me in about three or four states, not that they really know who I am."

"You are a sick bastard; that is who you are," Irina now took the step forward that Gavin dared not take, but she waited as Dorian finished his tale, instinctively curious as to how it might end.

Dorian ignored her completely, as if she weren't there. And, Gavin supposed, in his mind, neither of them was. In a few moments they would be wiped from the earth, forgotten and meaningless.

"From that point on, I couldn't really hang about in one place for too long. Always dangers around— that's why I only spent eight months at The Palace, of course. Normally, I would've just gotten out, made for state lines, but Kaylyn became a problem. See, issue with Kaylyn was, I actually *did* like her. So, I couldn't just leave her behind.

"I had the whole thing mapped out: we'd move to Europe, start over, I'd be basically untraceable. And, it would have worked perfectly. If Kaylyn had been willing to move to Europe. But the trouble was: she didn't want to leave her friends and family behind. Such a chore, to have to deal with someone like that, wouldn't you say?"

"So, you killed all her friends," Gavin extrapolated. "So she wouldn't have any ties to this place anymore."

"Don't forget about her family." Dorian winked.

"The drive-by shooting," Gavin remembered. "So, they weren't innocent bystanders."

"I must say, I even surprised myself with that one. Thought it would take at least three, four, five shots to get them both. But straight in the head, one after the other." He aimed an air gun at Irina. "Bang." At Gavin. "Bang."

"You did it all. You killed them all," Irina repeated, partially to the room, partially to herself.

"And when Kaylyn found out about your big plan"—Gavin tensed—"you had to kill her, too."

At this, Dorian paused, mouth open, considering. "Not quite…"

But he didn't have a chance to finish the thought. Irina took another step forward now and Gavin reached out to grab her, but he was too late. "You killed my boyfriend! You killed my boyfriend, and now, I kill you!" She charged forward, knife raised high and ready to plunge through the skin of their enemy.

Dorian's expression did not change, nor did he show any signs of rush or panic. As she took off for where he stood, on the other side of the room, Dorian simply waited. Waited for her to be close enough that she could not turn back.

And with a quick turn, he grabbed the frame of one of the motivational posters off the wall and brought it down mercilessly atop Irina's head. The glass shattered and flew wildly across the floor as Irina's body pressed through it, down to the shoulders.

Her arms were ensnared within the frame and the knife fell pathetically from her hand. She could have wriggled her way out and continued with her planned assault. But the blow had dazed her and, for a moment, everything became a blur.

As she struggled for consciousness, Dorian bent and casually selected a large, pointed shard of glass.

And, without hesitating, he drove it hard through Irina's falcon eye.

30. Presence

EVERYTHING WAS COLD. So cold that pain didn't even feel like pain anymore, more like the memory of a pain, long since gone, but never to be forgotten. The pieces were all there but none of them worked quite the way they once had. They still thought they could, however, and commanded that they be treated as such.

In the darkness, it was hard to tell whether it was lack of light or lack of sight that created the enveloping darkness all around. Or, perhaps, it was some combination of the two, bringing death in slow shades of fading. Because, by all accounts, Travis *should* have been dead. *Must* have been dead, he thought to himself, amazed that he could think.

He'd broken through the rotted boards with speed and momentum; he'd fallen so far that he could not recognize time; he'd struck the ground with such force that his head should have split on contact; and this was all secondary to the jagged wood that encircled him, spears ready to pierce the skin of even the most calloused body.

Yet, as he awoke, even the laceration on his head from where he'd smashed it into the bed as Dorian had grabbed for him seemed to have scabbed over. Or, he considered, had frozen shut.

How long had he been there? If he could still see, then it was still the night. But that didn't mean much. The nights were long in November. And there was no telling that this was the same night as the one on which he'd fallen.

He tried to blink, felt fairly certain that his eyelids *were* doing something. But he couldn't quite be sure.

What about his arms, his legs? Did they still operate as they once had? Or, at least, in some form at all? This was the first moment that he forced his brain to concentrate upon where his body parts actually *were*. And the thought of that sickened him enough that he tried to press it from his mind.

His right leg was bent beneath his body and turned at the knee. His left had caught on a cracked wooden board that jutted upright through the dirt, held up in a C-formation above his back.

His left arm was twisted, the shoulder separated, but this was the first part of his body that he seemed to be able to move, albeit, with minimal feeling. His right arm, on the other hand, was not worth speaking of. It had been turned so violently around that it now seemed to hang on by a few weak pieces of cartilage. While it didn't seem to have come detached altogether, it also did not seem that it would take much effort to finish the job.

Curling the fingers of his left hand was an effort, and it became a game, a chance to prove to himself that he was still alive and capable. If he could just get that index finger down. Then the middle. Ring and pinkie came as one. And the thumb. *Damn it, go down!*

It did. He had function. He had blood flow, slowly carrying some type of alleged warmth through the mistreated appendage, though his blood was cold as steel on a winter's eve. Next came his legs.

He tried the left first, certain that it would have snapped in two in its bent position. It would not move, could not lift nor fall. But, at the same time, it did not feel pain, not even in the numb and hollow manner of the rest of his aches.

He *could* feel it though. He pressed and thought, willed his brain into action. And, as his pant leg tore free from the jagged wood, he found that, incredibly, he had full range of motion from that side of his body.

The right leg would not be so simple. It moved— yes, it would move—but not in the direction he told it to. Not without daggers of pain searing through every nerve. Even the cold stopped numbing him as he tried to extract that dead appendage from beneath himself.

But he didn't have time for pain, nor for recovery. The more that his brain returned to life, the more pressure he felt to run, to seek his vengeance, and to finish what he'd started.

He rolled himself gingerly onto his right side, eyes squeezed tightly in agony. "Argh!" He grunted as sweat started to form on his head, even in this merci- less cold. Three deep, heavy breaths. Then, his heart started to slow to a steadier pump, his body coming to life once again.

That was the moment that a flicker of light shot across his eyelids. So, he could still see. Which would have been a relief if he knew precisely what he was seeing.

Although, somehow, he did know.

He peeled his eyes open slowly, blinking away the blurriness of his half-alive brain. And his sight fixed upon the wispy, translucent light of a faded, white foot. He followed the body up slowly to where Mav stood, head angled down at him, but eyes obscured by a crooked blindfold.

Behind him walked the ghost of Mallory, equally blindfolded, shaking as she stepped forward slowly, unseeingly, mouth starting to open in an eternal scream, though no sound came out.

As Travis squinted into the blackness, heart starting to race, once again, he watched as Kaylyn slowly faded into being, seated casually across the other side of a jagged terrain of broken wood and poisonous mushrooms. Though she, too, could not see from behind the blindfold that obscured her eyes, her finger picked lazily, curiously at the flaps of flesh that hung from her neck.

Indeed, all their necks were slashed, as in life, though none seemed too troubled to keep their heads upright as they looked down at him. Or, did they see him at all?

Travis opened his mouth, wanting to say something, or maybe just wanting to cry it all away, and every movement stopped. The ghosts became so impossibly still that they could have been statues erected to usher in the night. If not for the fact that he could see through them, could see them fading away.

"Now what?" he finally managed.

The ghosts were still; the air was only getting colder.

Then, Mav turned his head. Slowly. Deliberately. He fixed his face off to the right, staring through his mask at something in the distance. A moment later, Mallory did the same.

But Kaylyn kept looking at him, now picking again at the flesh of her neck. Reminding him that he could not stay here much longer, that he was not safe, here.

Travis pushed himself upward—the fire in his right leg trying to sway him down, straight at Mav. Straight through him? Travis didn't know what would happen if he came into contact with one of these ethereal figures of death, but something told him that he did not want to find out.

His half-good left arm swung out for a rotten two-by-four that crumbled under his weight, but he managed to get enough momentum from his initial pull that he was able to remain upright.

Travis staggered through the mud, the dampness of the soil pushing through his socks and weighing down his every step. Where the escape was—if there was an escape—he could not know. All he could do was follow the gazes of his deceased friends and hope, hope that they wouldn't lead him astray, though he did not know why they would help.

As he crossed past Mallory, she reached forward, as if to grab him, and he barely eluded her grasp. He whipped his head around to see her mouthing some-thing imperceptible. They all were. In unison. Chant-ing in their dead voices, inaudible to the human ear. It seemed like a warning. It could have been a threat. But, whatever it was, he was destined never to know.

Travis turned from them and ran, ran as fast as his one good leg would allow, hobbling through the dirt, cutting himself across wood that would surely leave infections in the morning. The further he went, the darker it got. His head struck against boards. The patio threatened to topple down atop him.

But, suddenly, the air felt fresher, freer. Though he could not see, just yet, he knew he had made it. The edge of the porch. He broke through the barrier and into the night, eyes gazing up at a skyful of stars. Almost there. He was almost there.

Before pressing onward, he turned back to where his former friends had stood, only to find a pure cave of darkness. They were gone, if they had ever been there.

He turned back, his path blocked by the faded fig-ures of Torri and Jim, sewn together by a single blind-fold that held them, back-to-back. His heart lurched as he stepped around them, but they made no move. They just stood, immobile, as if waiting to be called. On the other side, in the black alley that he needed to traverse, he flailed out to find the wall, connecting with nothing but air. He was going to fall. He could not keep going much longer.

His fingers made contact.

Relieved, he dragged himself along the brick, let-ting it cut into his fingers as he curled his way around the side of the house and, finally, reached the front.

The luminescence of what remained from an ex-plosive flame led Travis past a burnt-out car that had crumbled the front of The Little Maple Cabin. He barely glanced back as he circled around it but, from the corner of his eye, he could have sworn that he saw the driver, poking his mangled, translucent head out the window, laughing and hollering in absolute silence, a tattered blindfold slipping slowly past his eyebrows.

The door was in sight now, though the steps threatened to be a challenge. The railing creaked and lurched under his pressure and he was ready for another collapse as it shook. Somehow, it held, just enough to take him to the front door. It was ajar, although the fading, solitary streetlight did not illuminate anything of the inside.

As he broke the threshold, he felt as though sound had returned to the air, but that sound was the hollow death of a thousand men and women. He stumbled forward a few steps to where Mick had sent him on his near-fatal flight. He was back again, head still in hand. But this time, he didn't block the path. His form slid aside, with hardly a movement, to let him pass. And, as he did so, he felt the cold, hollow soul of the young, dead man clawing at his own.

The kerosene lamp that burned down its last vestiges of fuel on the living room table summoned him, past where Brady dangled lifelessly from the ceiling, now hanged by the neck, his blindfold so loose it was nearly falling off. Travis tried not to look at the dark chasm in the side of his head, but couldn't keep his eyes away. Until Brady's head lurched in the noose, turning to face him, the blindfold coming ever closer to slipping down.

Travis shut his eyes and made for the lamp, only to find another hand reaching for it, simultaneously.

He pulled back just in time to avoid contact with Malachi, or what he had to assume was Malachi, for this spectre was flaked in darkness, the white glow around him consumed by the black specks of melting, contorted skin. The blindfold stuck to his hollow skull of a head, matted to the bubbled skin. Malachi's hand carried straight through the handle of the lamp and into the flame itself, which licked at his skeletal fingers until the light went out and left Travis alone in the darkness.

He whipped around, as the silence of the dead grew louder, pressuring his eardrums and threatening to push them in. No matter what direction he turned in, he could not escape, could not see an exit. He became disoriented. Pain thrust through his body and he wanted to cry out, but his voice was not allowed to come, not anymore.

Dizzy, on the verge of vomiting, he dropped down upon his good knee and bowed his head, begging the ghosts to give him some moment of peace, some chance to finish.

And then, from the corner of the room, he saw the pale, translucent head of Irina poke above the landing as she slowly ascended the stairs, her blindfold a thin strip of lace, nearly see-through, one dark hole threatening to suck him in from behind the cloth. A shard of glass protruded from the other eye, straight through the lace.

"You, too?" he whispered to himself, rising slowly, stumbling, forcing himself up. He paced cautiously toward the ghost, knowing that the basement was his inevitable destination.

Irina raised a hand as he neared, and he feared that she would grab him, push him down to his death. But instead, in some ways, much, much worse, she reached up for the shard of glass, small black trickles of what must have been ghostly blood beading upon her hand as she wriggled the jagged edge around, trying to pull it away, a long stream of blood now snaking its way down her face.

Travis tried not to look at her, tried not to feel the frigid aura that surrounded her as he passed onto the stairs.

And the moment that he took the first step, he felt a release. The silence of the dead disappeared into absolute silence, as quickly as if no change had ever occurred. He did not need to look. He could feel that Irina was gone, behind him.

He took the stairs slowly. He could move no other way. As he pressed forward, seeking the dim, flickering light that awaited him below, he slid his hand into the waistband of his jeans, carefully removing the peeling knife he'd lifted from the block while they had all been drinking scotch in the kitchen. The knife that, miraculously, had not sliced through him during his fall. And with that, he knew, in one way or another, this would be the end of his journey.

31. Back

DORIAN BRUSHED IRINA out of the way with the side of his foot, such a light touch that it seemed almost impossible how easily she rolled to the side, her blood-drenched face looking up to the Heaven her dark soul would never see.

In one fluid motion. Dorian ducked down and snatched up the knife that she'd dropped upon her collapse and inspected it closely. "Basic chef's knife. A classic weapon of choice, but a bit long for my tastes. I like to have a little more dexterity, make sure I hit the right spot." He looked up from the knife to raise an eyebrow at Gavin. "Not to mention that there's always something just a little more…personal…about finishing the job right up close." Gavin swallowed hard, but could not speak. "There's something to be said for honour and respect, even in killing, wouldn't you say? You owe the other at least the *chance* to look you in the eye, to feel your breath upon their skin and theirs on yours, as you take the only thing that really matters to them. It's just polite." He smiled, no longer trying to hold back the cruelty in his expression. "But this will have to do."

Gavin took a step away, angled his body so that his back now faced the stairs. If he could jump, get a head start, then maybe he'd be able to get away, head straight for the door, keep on running into the night. The rest, he'd figure out later. He was pretty sure that, if he dropped the dead weight of the lamp, he'd be able to find the front door in the dark. But he needed a few more steps on Dorian before he took his chance. Dorian may not have been an athlete—although, Gavin really couldn't say for sure, one way or the other—but his legs were longer, and Gavin was sorely out of shape.

A few more steps. Then he'd feel semi-confident that he could at least beat Dorian to the top of the stairs and, from there, he'd be able to pick up momentum on the straightaway into the forest.

But it seemed as though Dorian was prepared for this possibility—or, at least, that he wasn't ready to let the gap between them become any wider. With each tiny inch that Gavin stole toward freedom, Dorian took two of his own, curling around the room along a separate axis.

"You don't have to do this," Gavin managed to choke out. "There's no need. Everyone else is dead. It's just me left and, at this point, they'll probably think that I did it. There's no record of you, right? They'll never know you were here. My word against the word of a ghost." He winced at his use of the term, even if it was only metaphorical. "Who're they gonna believe?"

"Or, alternatively,"—Dorian held the knife loosely, casually, like it was a cigarette rather than a deadly weapon—"we could just wipe clean all memory of me being here. And, by the time they find you all, I'll be weeks, if not months, away."

"You're forgetting about the house's owner," Gavin bluffed, remembering that Dorian hadn't seen the crash, praying that he would panic. "That DJ guy.

He'll be up to clean tomorrow and I'm pretty sure he'll tell someone."

Dorian scoffed, throwing his head back in false laughter. Gavin tried to take this chance to move a full two steps toward the stairs but, even without looking, Dorian shifted with him. "It's a good try, I'll give you that. But you don't think I don't know what that crash was, do you? I'm not stupid enough to forget the only other person who knows the exact address we're at."

Gavin deflated. "It was you. You cut the brakes."

"Well, I wasn't actually going to go into town to find a couple of cops to come and arrest me. I had to do something with my time. To be honest, I thought for sure you three were going to catch me in the act when you went to visit the guy, but I guess it was too dark to see my car parked down the street."

"You were there?"

"The whole time. Had to wait for you to get home before I could drive back, of course. Couldn't have you see me coming in from the wrong direction. To be honest, I thought for sure you'd figure out something was up when I told that cock-and-bull story about the police station being closed." He laughed, for real this time. "Honestly, all the emergency services in town were closed? You just *believed* that?"

Gavin blamed himself, although they'd all fallen for it in the same way. It should have been obvious, though, now that he heard it aloud. "It just seemed like…like anything was possible out here."

Dorian smiled his cruel, sick smile once again, but it didn't last for long. His eyes opened slightly wider as the corners of his lips turned down, as if in slow motion, mouth cracking ever-so-slightly open in a curious showing of amazement. Gavin furrowed his brow as his body went cold. "What?" he managed in a hoarse whisper, starting to shake from a frigid sensation that was washing over him.

Dorian shook his head slowly, wonder still breaking through his expression. "Well, I'll be damned. It looks like you weren't wrong, Gav." And Gavin couldn't help but cringe at the diminutive of his name coming from the mouth of a monster. "Anything *can* happen out here."

"What are you…?" he began, but he never got to finish.

Behind him, Travis trudged slowly but surely across the long path of basement to where they stood, his dead leg dragging behind him yet making almost no sound in the bleak vacuum of the house. It was Dorian's turn to take a step backward, disbelief hitting him with more force than fear for his safety.

Travis held the peeling knife high in his left hand, curved blade pointed and angry, ready to attack.

A few more feet. His shoulder tensed; his eyes widened in preparation for the final blow.

And with a vicious, careless lunge, the most forceful assault he could manage beneath the shackles of his mangled body, Travis drove the knife forward with merciless passion.

Straight into the heart of Gavin's back.

He never knew what hit him. Never knew that his one-time friend had even been in the room. Eyes still fixed on Dorian, the last sight that his living eyes would ever see, Gavin buckled to his knees, nearly dragging Travis down with him.

His mouth opened wide and he tried to say something, to ask what had happened, but all that came out was a thick, steady stream of viscous, red blood.

Stutter-stepping to keep his feet, Travis yanked the knife violently from Gavin's flesh, sending a steady pump of blood flowing through the young man's shirt. Then, he pitched forward, face striking hard into the ground with a crunch of bone that he would, blissfully, never feel.

For a moment, Travis stared at his victim, battling down his remorse and channeling all emotion into pity for his poor friend, whom he had wished, least of all, to have to kill. But he was interrupted in his inconsequential payment of respects by a slow clap commencing crudely from the other side of the room.

"Well, well, well." Dorian's smile returned, along with a brief chuckle. "So. You're the other one, huh? That bump on the head must have done you in good."

Travis raised his eyes slowly to face the killer across the room, hatred burning passionately through his blood as he took in Dorian's laissez-faire posture and casual grip on the slick blade in his hands.

"I never thought it made sense it was you," Travis mumbled, mostly to himself. "But none of the rest seemed right. At least not after we proved it wasn't Irina."

"Well, I can't say I much suspected you, either." Dorian ceased his ironic applause and tightened his grip upon the knife, now pointing it at Travis as he carried on. "I just couldn't figure out *why* you'd do it."

"Then go on wondering," Travis shot back in a gravelly, sickly tone, eyes drifting away in disassociation from one he refused to put himself on a level with, the day's actions aside.

"Oh, come on," Dorian nagged. "You might as well tell me at this point." Travis turned his eyes back to Dorian, sizing him up, wondering if he had the strength to take him, should it come to it. No—*when* it came to it.

"Why do you even care?"

"Call it a dying man's last wish." He smirked.

"Not a lot of confidence in yourself, then?"

"Win or lose, I die tonight, Travis. Whether it's a corporeal death or a spiritual one. Tomorrow, I'm going to be as far away from this place as possible. I don't just want to get away: I need to. I need to disappear. To be somewhere safe, where I'll never be found. And, I suppose, you really ought to do the same."

"I'm not going anywhere."

"I think that's for the fates to decide. In the meantime, why not regale me with the tale of your twisted little mind." Travis looked away again, contemplatively, before shooting his gaze back up, intently boring through Dorian's perverse, crooked grin. "Oh, come on. It doesn't matter now," Dorian pressed, once again. "After all, in just a few very, very

short minutes, there will only be one of us left to remember the story, anyway."

32. Appearances

"THEY WERE MY friends." Travis looked down, forlornly, at Gavin's folded corpse upon the floor, blood still spreading its final fingers out around the gash in the back of his shirt. "I didn't want to kill them. I *really* didn't."

"But, sometimes, you do what needs to be done," Dorian finished, understandingly. So understandingly that it made Travis sick, for he barely understood, himself.

"They were—they *could have been*—in the way. They almost were. I swear, the thought crossed my mind weeks ago but it was just for a second. I even got mad at myself for thinking it. Then, I told myself it was all a joke, just a stupid passing idea to laugh at but never to actually do. But then, yesterday, last night…" He drifted away as he spoke, everything flickering back into his head with hazy edges, scarring at his mind: Gavin's stupid little quip by the beer pong table about how he was a cheater, Kaylyn's open chastisement in the kitchen, so very nearly over-heard.

"I love Alyssa," he began, the present tense lost upon neither of them. "I *really* love Alyssa. And I fought hard to get her, to make her love me back. You understand how hard that can be, when someone just puts her hand around your heart and squeezes without even knowing she did it, and then won't let go even as her words say she isn't interested? It took me two years to get her to date me. And the last three years—it was perfect. It was everything I imagined it would be."

"You cheated on her, didn't you?" Dorian may have been cruel, may have been sick, but he was quick, Travis had to give him that.

Travis thought about equivocating, trying to make himself out as well as he could before carrying on, but there was no point. He didn't need to sell himself to a joker. "Yes. I cheated on her. Several times with several women. And I never regretted it for a second."

Dorian smirked, toying with the tip of his knife, turning it around its axis against the pad of his index finger, as though it was a toy, as though he didn't notice the tiny bead of blood that was slowly manifesting there, waiting for gravity's call to ease down the cool edge of the stainless-steel track. "Yet, you say you were in love with her."

"It's not the same thing," Travis snapped, defensively.

"Okay, testy-testy, are we? Forgive me if your claims don't completely make sense. I'm sure some would say the same of mine." He absently tapped Irina's face with his toe, the shard of glass still penetrating her eye wriggling upon his touch and easing its way out to the ground below, leaving the open gash that chasmed into her skull staring out at them.

"I love Alyssa," Travis repeated. "But love isn't sex. I was a football player; I was *popular*, if that matters. I had girls whenever I wanted them for so long, but none of them meant anything to me. They were fun, and they knew the game. I never led anyone on.

We both got what we wanted and that was the end of it. Alyssa was different. It wasn't a game. That was life. But just because you're settled in life doesn't mean you have to stop playing."

"Except, it does." Dorian raised his eyebrows.

"Except, sometimes, it does," Travis conceded. "They were fun; they were drunken ends to party nights. But that was all they were."

"But Alyssa saw differently."

"Presumably."

"So, she never found out?"

Travis looked down to Gavin once again, a note of sadness wafting across his visage. "No. But they did." He took a breath as he recalled the worst decision of his life. "I wasn't even thinking about it. Why would I? I was hanging out with Gavin and Mav, Kaylyn and Mallory, like we always did. Just drinking and playing some games back at my place. Game's on an app and Gavin wants to see the settings. I hand him my phone and, of course, at that moment, one of those stupid hookups decides to text me. Incriminating stuff.

"And Gavin, being Gavin, being unable to process anything without flipping out over it, reads it out loud to everyone. Obviously, I told them what I'm telling you, about how it's just sex and nothing else. That I really *do* love Alyssa and none of that's a lie. Gavin accepted that, and so did Mav, figured they were more my friend than Alyssa's anyway, so there was no point in blowing up a friendship over someone they didn't care about as much. But Kaylyn was different."

"She'd been cheated on before," Dorian mused. "She told me. Broke her 'for years', she said. Couldn't trust 'dirty, stupid men anymore.' At least, until I came around." He grinned.

"Yeah." Travis gritted his teeth. "She really had great taste."

"She threatened to tell, of course," Dorian concluded.

"Yes and no," Travis sighed. "Basically, but she didn't make it that simple. Gavin and Mav tried to convince her that my logic was sound and that there was a difference between cheating physically and cheating emotionally. She wasn't hearing it, but she accepted the 'he's more our friend than she is' argument. At least, partly. She threatened to tell Alyssa, but with a caveat: she wouldn't say anything if I stopped altogether. Still kept pressuring me to say something, but if I could stay clean—no more hookups, no more cheating. Cold turkey. Just be a good and loyal boyfriend for the rest of time and she wouldn't say a word. But, if I couldn't do that, she couldn't be friends with me anymore, couldn't be friends with a cheater. And then, she'd tell Alyssa."

"And Mallory?"

Travis shook his head disapprovingly. "Just followed along with anything Kaylyn said, of course."

"Of course," Dorian acknowledged from experience. "So…" He set his deep blue eyes intently upon Travis. "You couldn't do it?"

Travis scoffed. "I told you: I love Alyssa. With everything I have. If that's what it took to keep the relationship alive, then that's what it took, end of story.

That was three months ago. I haven't cheated since. Was never going to again. It may have been irritating, that they didn't understand, but I didn't have to think about it too hard once the terms were set out in front of me."

Dorian furrowed his brow, stroking his chin with his bloody finger, drawing the red across his face as though he didn't realize it was there. "But then…why'd you have to kill them? Just because they posed a theoretical threat to your relationship? I mean, I understand love, trust me. I did all of this"— he gestured about himself as though it was some kind of great triumph—"just for Kaylyn. But I'm a special breed and you just don't seem the type…"

"It was more than just the relationship," Travis admitted.

"Even after Alyssa was gone?" The words stung Travis but he ignored them. "Why still kill Kaylyn and Gavin when it didn't matter anymore, when she couldn't find out."

Travis ignored him. "Anyway, it was my entire future that mattered. Not just that." He took a deep breath, not wanting to hear what he knew he was going to have to say. He tried to remind himself that one of them would be dead soon, and none of this would matter, but that didn't make it any easier. "Did Kaylyn tell you anything about my family?"

"Kaylyn barely talked about anything but herself. It was one of her most endearing traits." Dorian smiled and suddenly Travis wondered whether this was the truth, or if Dorian simply wanted to force Travis to say what he didn't want to say.

"Suffice it to say, they're a bunch of alcoholics, thieves, and pyramid scheme victims. I don't come from much, and that's why I was stuck working at The Palace instead of going to school, like I wanted. The grades were there, but not the money. And I'm not taking out a loan I can never repay."

"A common story." Dorian almost looked bored.

"But that's not why Alyssa was working there."

Something clicked. "Right. The poor little rich girl, sent off by her family to earn a living."

"To learn what hard work is like. But never to go unsupported. She has the money, but not the grades. And her family likes me…"

"You became the surrogate child."

"I'm not going to go that far but, a couple of months ago, her dad was talking to me about paying my way through college. Giving me the opportunity I was never going to have, otherwise. I couldn't take any chances that it would get out, regardless of…*anything* else."

Dorian hummed, now twirling his knife along the back of the couch and watching a spurt of stuffing burst from the seams. Destruction for destruction's sake, at this point. "It makes sense. I'll accept it. Although, I'm surprised you trusted your friends so little. *Especially* after they'd all promised not to tell. Not really friends, then, were they? Conveniences to have around that suddenly became inconvenient."

Travis shook his head. "I didn't want to do it. I didn't *intend* to do it. But last night—last night, when they were drinking, they almost let it slip, multiple times. I just—I realized that no matter how sound their promises were, as long as they knew, they'd always be liabilities. They'd always pose a risk to my future.

"And then other people started dying and…and, I guess, I saw my chance. Take them out and blame it on the ghost, or whoever the hell caused the rest of this mayhem. Then, walk away. Free from risk. Move on."

"Last second with the first weapon you could find. No wonder your killings were so…*uninspired*."

"It's not an art," he spat back at Dorian. "It's the worst thing I could possibly have done. And I'd do it again, but I'd *never* do it for fun."

Dorian shrugged. "To each his own." That unnerving and perverse smile crept back onto his face. "I guess," he continued, digging the knife a little deeper into the couch. "I just have one more question for you. There's one more thing that…just…no matter how hard I think about it, I just can't make sense of it at all…

"You say you loved Alyssa, that you wanted to protect your relationship, that you did all of this killing for her. So, I just can't wrap my head around…why you killed her."

Travis hesitated, the peeling knife slipping slightly in his grip as his elbow tensed. Nearly released. He swallowed slowly, staring hard into Dorian's eyes as he felt the blood begin to pump faster through his veins. His head throbbed and he felt a slow storm of blood beginning to flow through the crack in his forehead, to make the stitches from his accident dehisce, to threaten to pour into his eyes. He felt faint, his jaw quivered.

His mouth struggled to form the words that he didn't know how to express, and that finally poured out of him in the weakest of voices, a tense and breathless squeak. "B-but…you killed Alyssa."

Dorian blinked once, and they proceeded to stare at each other, hard and immobile, each trying to call a bluff that the other had not made, trying to see through the eyes of his rival with nothing left to read but a cold, blank stare.

At first, it seemed that Gavin's kerosene lamp, lying on its side on the floor in front of him, had started to glow brighter and brighter, until it became blinding. They would have thought the room had caught fire, if not for the fact that the direction was wrong. The light didn't blaze between them, but beside them, from the corner of the room, just a few feet away from the door that refused to open.

Neither wanting to be distracted from the weapon of the other, but equally unable to keep themselves from the increasing intensity, they turned in unison to face what vision had appeared before them. At first, the light glowed too brightly for them to make anything out. They fell blind, so unused to the light but now wishing that they'd never begged for it back.

Instinctively, they wanted to take a step backward, but they were unable to move. Not just shocked into immobility, but physically knitted to their places. Blinking away the glare, they squinted through the white; a white that seemed to grow and creep closer, closer to them as they waited.

And just as quickly as it had grown, it began to fade away, leaving something standing behind, a silhouette in the dark. Standing perfectly still.

33. Manifest

AT FIRST, SHE didn't move, body frozen in the profound darkness that accompanied the light's fade. But she was still visible, white—tinged slightly golden—her hair billowing behind her, as fluttered the clothes upon her body.

Or, on what *had* been her body, for Alyssa was no longer herself, no longer a physical being, but a spectre of the light, the angel in chains, whose descent upon the earth was both a gift upon the eyes of all who beheld her, yet a pox upon those who dared to steal a look.

The room was no longer cold. Rather, an intense warmth had pervaded the space, cutting away all other feeling or focus but for that directed toward her. But it was not the heat of Malachi's fire, nor of the kerosene lamp that now died at their feet. It was the warmth of an embrace, soft and tender, that clasped the cheek to the bosom of hope and destiny in the peaceful promise of protection.

Until that embrace became a little too tight, squeezed, refused to let go. Suddenly, they felt as though they were suffocated by it. Now, unable to move, speak, or breathe. And Alyssa, like them, could do nothing but stand, eyes to the sky, unaware of her surroundings or of the spectacle that was herself.

The billowing stopped and, for a moment, air seemed to breathe back into the room. She was still but, somehow, awake, ready, and everything but alive.

Slowly, as if creaking on an ancient, unused axis, her chin lowered from its raised position and drew her face down, bit by bit, to face Travis and Dorian.

In that moment, she was beautiful, a fleeting taste of the Heaven that awaited, extending a generous hand down to Earth and impressing upon mere mortals what no living soul was ever designed to know. Together, Travis and Dorian sucked in their first breaths in what felt like several minutes, though it had been just a few seconds, in reality.

And they stared at her, into her, took in what she offered so effortlessly, so impossibly. Until they stared for too long.

The closer they looked upon the angel who hung before them, feet slightly raised from the ground, fingers and toes pointed to the floor, the more that something felt wrong about the exchange. More wrong than the presence of a ghostly figure in the heart of the basement.

And though she dragged them in, made them want to be consumed, something screamed in their ears in Alyssa's voice, a meek bell in the otherwise heavy static of their brains. They needed to run like hell.

Then the angel came forth. Drifted. Easing her way above the ground toward them. A wash of sadness, of loss, penetrated both of them until their stomachs knotted and their necks tightened. They were free to move once more, liberated at the first movement permitted to the vision before them. But, now, it was shock that held them in place. And wonder. The irrepressible desire to know what in the world was destined to happen when she arrived at her destination.

The closer she came, the more that the aura started to fade away, bringing her gold-and-white features into the clear. Her chin as soft and tight as ever, her cheekbones high, yet smooth, her nose rounded into a small, fragile wave. But gone were the deep cerulean eyes that she had worn so well. Replaced, instead, by gouged holes, black and hollow as the night, surrounded by stringy veins and cracks that seemed to carve around her head and to grow as she approached, the fissure widening, widening to suck them in.

To suck Travis in.

The embodiment that once was Alyssa had turned specifically upon her former lover, her false lover, and approached, now, with the blood-red force of Hell at her core. Her fingers reached out as her nails chipped away before him, stretching for his neck, ready to drive straight through him.

Travis tried to back up, but he could not run, could barely turn away. As horrible and monstrous as this Alyssa was, he could not drop his gaze. Her fingers were inches away now, ready to make contact and to bring, with that other-worldly touch, the final consumption of Travis' living soul.

Travis found the breath to cry out, to try to beat himself away, but she had his arms now, locked into place and going cold beneath her burning grasp. And the louder he screamed, the louder she screamed, as well, her voice crying out in low, heart-crushing tones, as those that had once rung out from behind the locked door. That *still* rang out from behind the locked door, joining in harmony with the bellows of both figures.

As she wailed, Alyssa's face began to crack away, consumed by whatever inhumanity designed her skeleton.

Travis felt himself becoming smaller under her touch, sinking into the ground where he stood and wishing that he had never woken up from his fall through the back porch, that he could remain in blissful silence in the cold, dark emptiness of the absent world.

The pain returned in full force to his leg, to his arm. Suddenly, his whole body felt crumpled and squeezed, returning him to the broken and mangled pose that he'd worn upon his fall. His shoulder separated, his leg bent and cracked, his knee inverted. And his skull tore apart from every gaping seam, dragging flesh from bone as she disembowelled him, his body seeming to turn inside out and the pieces that had kept him alive pouring out into a mess of himself on the floor.

And still, she gripped hard, digging in tighter, with hands that had no form and could not touch, but that could violate without a moment's pause. Her face pressed closer to his, as it had so many times when she had nuzzled her head into his neck, cuddled up close for warmth. But she wasn't here for comfort, this time. Her cracked mouth open, wider still, her scream ongoing even after Travis' ability to cry out had long since been rent from his body and thrust away into the winds of night, she pressed forth to consume him whole, to suck him into her bodiless body and erase what little worth he had from the world and from memory.

Travis ceased feeling pain, yet this was somehow worse than pain, because in the absence of all that he knew and understood, he was faced with silence, so loud in its death, that he could not hear anything but that audial vacuum.

And Dorian stood, rooted in place, as he watched Travis sucked into Alyssa, as she grew brighter and stronger. And much, much crueller. The air was heavy with anger and pain. And as Travis' blood dripped listlessly down her incorporeal lips, Alyssa's hollow eyes that seemed to be and eat the night, simultaneously, curled up from the prey she sucked deep into her depths and looked to and through Dorian. The unspoken threat of 'you're next' blistering through his immobile core.

But not immobile—no—he thought he was; he could've been sure of it. Because he couldn't feel a thing, his entire body rotted away and disconnected from the brain that took in everything it saw but understood nothing of it, aside from its gravity. But he was shaking. He suddenly became aware that, although he couldn't feel it, he was shaking. It was the only explanation for the blur around his eyes, the lack of clarity that he could not blink away.

His brain told his legs to run and he found himself moving, somehow, through the basement halls, just as Alyssa completed her destruction of her victimizer and looked up to face him. She did not pursue, however, as her body faded into the night. But as she disappeared into the ether, to walk these halls eternally, she took with her all light and heat that had, so briefly, provided comprehensibility to the room.

Dorian broke in fear, yelping out as he flew over a couch in the darkness, smacking his head upon the hardwood floor and slipping as he tried to regain his footing. No time to reset, he continued his attempt forward, aware that he was upright, but unable to conceive of whether he was actually getting anywhere in the black.

And then he was ascending. Beautifully, incredibly, he'd found the stairs and was shooting up toward safety, toward his car, which still sat where he'd left it, waiting for him, just beyond the front door.

Tears of relief stung through his eyes and he blinked them away as he burst onto the landing, the dim glow of the single streetlamp through the open front door providing him with vision once again. So blinded, he was, by his influx of calm, that he didn't notice the dangling legs of Brady, nearly striking him as he passed.

He curled back, toward the front door, sliding on the wood, banging his knee into the ground and cursing, before jumping back up and shooting forward. Until Mick peeled himself away from the wall to block his killer's path.

Dorian skidded to a stop, falling backward and striking the back of his head on the floor upon impact. As he looked up at Mick, eyes wide in horror, the decapitated man slowly took his head in both of his hands and held it out toward Dorian. Not an offering, but a presentation. *See what you have done?*

Dorian pressed up with his arms and crab-walked backward, losing balance and falling before pushing up and crab-walking again. And Mick pursued, slowly, one heavy step at a time. There was no choice but to run.

Dorian rolled and, just as Mick's outstretched hand was about to grip his ankle, he leapt up and turned for the kitchen, the garage. There had to be a way out through there, through a hole in the wall. He would make one if he had to.

But, the moment he opened the door, he found himself face-to-face with the charred, translucent remains of Malachi, who reached one blackened claw forward for Dorian's neck as the killer slammed the door, just in time to be saved. The arm protruded through the wood, still reaching blindly for him.

Dorian backed into the kitchen island, striking his back hard, but ignoring the sear of pain. He glanced to his left and saw that Mick had stopped pursuing, but he still stood in the path, awaiting Dorian's return, Brady's dangling body turning upon its rope, next to him, to face Dorian and go rigid, head snapping up to watch him as he ran.

The back porch. He would have to chance it. Let the fall be damned, he would come prepared for it. He crossed the room at a run and grasped the handle, still unlocked from when he had closed it last.

But the moment he looked up, he stopped. Torri and Jim idled upon the porch, somehow standing upon the unstable ground, safe from the weight of the human fall. And they glided in unison toward him.

He slammed the glass door shut and broke back to the stairs. There had to be a window he could lift himself through.

Or, at least, a place where he could hide until morning.

He blew past Mick and Brady, who reached for him, ghostly fingers just grazing the edge of his shirt and sending a cold shock through Dorian's body, so incomprehensible that it sent him plummeting down into the darkness below.

But not complete darkness, he found, as he shook his head and groaned the pain in every body part away. Across the room, Irina stood over her corpse, looking down upon it, the white light of her form drawing him in like a moth. He resisted, looked back up the stairs.

But at the top, they all waited. Every body he had corrupted, standing patiently for his return, so that they could repay the favour. He pressed along the wall of the basement, as quietly as he could, hoping, absurdly, that maybe Irina wouldn't know that he was there, if he could just be stealthily silent.

But no sound mattered to a spectre. She could feel his presence. Her head shot around from where she had been staring down, and her blindfold began to fall away, no longer held in place by the shard of glass that Dorian had kicked free.

Her dark, hollow chasms stared back at him, sucking him in.

He closed his eyes and turned left, begging that she would not pursue but knowing that he could not be so fortunate. His knee crashed into the low side table and sent him sprawling to the ground along with broken wood. He clambered to his hands and knees and looked back over his shoulder to the menagerie of ghosts that had formed a semicircle around him, now. All of their blindfolds had slipped away. Mick, Brady, Torri, Jim, Malachi, and Irina. Hollow chasm eyes, drawing him in, threatening to take him, much as Alyssa had taken Travis. But without the warmth, without the gold.

These were no angels and their revenge would not be so glorious.

They trekked in unison, one translucent foot after the other, closing him in against the wall behind him as he scrambled to his feet and pressed hard against the wood, praying that he could disappear.

"No, please, no!" he blubbered, in infantile desperation. "No! Everyone, please! Please, everyone, let me go!"

A scream wailed out through the room, seeming to travel through Dorian's body and shaking his insides. It emanated from behind the locked door, the door that was right behind him. The only place he could go.

He whirled around and threw all his force into that handle, jamming and turning, peering over his shoulder to see how near they had come. They were closing in fast, though they moved so slowly. They had all the time in eternity, and he had only a few moments before he was consumed.

Dorian banged a fist into the door, begging that he could get away, disappear, be as far as possible

from this place. He threw himself into it, again and
again.

And then, the ghosts just inches behind him, he
thrust forward one, final time, and fell through into
the black.

34. Disappear

DORIAN DID NOT know how long he'd been falling, nor whether he was falling at all. The world around him was black and empty, with no clear sense of direction or gravity. Up, down, he could not know. He, simply, was and was not.

After a while, he began walking and discovered that he was upright. Perhaps he had been all along. The ground beneath him did not feel firm, nor present, but it held him, or so he thought, anyway.

He tried to turn back to the world from whence he'd come but could not identify it in the darkness. But, somehow, *darkness* didn't feel quite right. It wasn't that the place was unlit so much as that this was what it was meant to look like. Walls upon walls of infinite black, a location that the sun did not know existed and where vision was perceptual, not physical.

Dorian was alone. All alone. He had disappeared.

He started to run, just to be sure, to beat around with his fingers in search of something tangible. Because, this could not be it. He was not meant to be gone altogether.

Was he dead? No, that didn't feel right. He'd seen the dead, felt their auras, their energies. This was not what they had felt like. They had had their own vibration, their own sound in the madness. But there was no vibration, here. This was the epitome of nothingness, the nadir of perception.

The further he ventured into his eternity, the closer he came to his end. Nothing was logical anymore. He sought to walk upward and found no concept of what that was. He stood on walls, on ceilings, all figments of his own mind, much as if the world, as a whole, were little more than the concept of an overworked brain.

But, as liberating as it was to be devoid of existence, if just for a few moments, this was not the goal, and he needed to escape. He had run from death and won the race, but he planned to drink from a champion's cup, not to be erased from history in the absence that was this room.

Because, this was a room. Yes, he reminded himself. As maddeningly impossible as it seemed to be, this was nothing more than the room behind the locked door, unlit and unseeable, but natural, all the same. He just had to find the other side of the door and open it. And, if it would not unlock, he would feel for the hinges and smash them away, turn the screws from the frame with his broken, bloody fingernails, if the need presented itself.

He just needed to find that door.

He could have walked for an hour or a minute, a day or a second. It was impossible to tell what was happening or where he was, or if there were a location that he could identify as 'where'. But there had to be. He knew that there must have been a way out.

A light appeared before him, white and glowing, but small upon the horizon of his eyes. As he walked, it grew and Dorian became aware, for the first time, of depth within the room. He pressed closer and closer until the figure came into clearer focus, and he laid his eyes, confusedly, upon a woman whom he did not recognize.

She was in her late-thirties or early-forties, but still possessed the smooth, clean beauty of youth. Her hair was brown or, at least, it *had* been brown before she became engulfed in the shades of black and white that now determined her existence. Her hands were well manicured, as were her toes. She wore no shoes beneath the long, flowing dress that she sat in.

She was facing him but did not see him. Her eyes were closed, and a jolt shot through Dorian at the thought of what might have lain behind those lids. She was humming, quietly, to herself, a tune with words he could not comprehend, but that she seemed to know by rote, as though she had been singing it for a long time.

Something about her voice was familiar, and it took him a few minutes to match it with the scream that had rung out from behind the locked door as Alyssa had consumed Travis before his eyes. But, she wasn't screaming now. In fact, she seemed al-most…peaceful…

"Hello?" he tried, but his voice didn't work on the first attempt. "Hello?" he managed, successfully, the second time.

With a start, her eyes shot open to look at him, and Dorian was relieved to see that she possessed full, once-light-brown eyes, and not chasms of darkness.

She reviewed him for a few moments, considering his presence with her lips slightly parted. Finally, she managed, "Who are you?"

"I was about to ask the same question."

She smiled a mischievous smile that buried something away and demanded that he guess at it.

She said nothing and looked down at her dress. She tore a strip away and plucked at a thread. A moment later, she was using her fingers, dextrously, to sew the strip back onto the rest of her clothing, using just her hands. So expert, she was, that it could only have been a habit, developed over decades upon decades of practice, with nothing better to do.

"Excuse me," Dorian began again, but her eyes shot back to him harshly and he knew to keep quiet. She carried about her business, humming her haunting tune, until the strip was reattached, as cleanly as if it had never been torn away.

Finally, she turned to Dorian again and said, softly, "My name is Vera Meadows. I used to live in the house that, if I'm not mistaken, you've just arrived from. But that was a long time ago."

"How long?" Dorian was not sure if he wanted to know the answer. She just smiled coyly. "What is this place?"

"This? This is the void. Welcome."

"B-but…how did we get here?"

Vera shrugged, lightly, daintily. "I don't know. I don't suppose anyone knows. It may have something to do with the curse my lover put upon this place. Or, perhaps, it simply awaits all those who run. You *were* running from something, were you not?" She raised her eyebrows and he felt, somehow, pierced by her soft eyes. The sensation was uncomfortable.

Dorian nodded once. "What were you running from?"

"My husband, naturally. Manny was a great man, but a terrible man. I don't know what would have happened if he'd caught me. But I'm glad that I got away. I believe—that is, I've listened to the world around, the one you've come from. He still walks those halls. Has he found his angel yet? I know he was searching for her. If he could not have me, then a surrogate."

Dorian swallowed hard but found that he'd lost the reflex to swallow. "Yeah, he found her," he whispered.

Vera smiled wanly, "Then, maybe, there will be peace now. So long as no more death befalls that house…but I can tell, from your expression, that this is not the case. A pity, really."

Dorian reached up to cover the lower half of his face, to process without giving himself away, but he was sent backward in shock by the sight of his hand, white and translucent before his eyes. In shock and wonder, he examined it closely. "You'll get used to that," Vera noted, returning to her ripping and sewing, ripping and sewing. "You have lots of time."

Dorian shook his head. He did not want time. He wanted out. "What now? What do we do, now?"

Vera chuckled lightly to herself. "What, indeed? What would you like?"

"To get out, to go back?"

She looked up at him again, a long and slow look, consideration brewing behind her pitying countenance. "There's no going back," she explained. "This is it."

"No. No!" Dorian backed away but didn't seem to get anywhere, at all. "I can't stay here. I don't want to be here! I want to be able to get out!"

"But, didn't you want to disappear, Dorian?" She rose; she knew him. She stepped forward as he fell back, or fell forward, or fell away. "Isn't this what you wanted? To get far away from where you were, from where the world could hurt you for what you'd done?"

She leaned in close as he spiralled away from himself, her figure seeming to envelop him in the white flow of her billowing dress. And she whispered in his ear, just before he fell back into the black, "We're safe here, Dorian. We're finally safe. They can't get us here. We've finally disappeared. Forget about getting out. That's not what you want.

"They'll never be able to get in."

AFTERWORD

Horror is my favourite genre. Maybe not so much when I was a young child, afraid to open my eyes in movie theatre halls or video rental stores in case I passed some scary cover art—sparked, if I recall correctly, by a poster for *Bride of Chucky* (Yu, 1998). When I got old enough for that initial terror to pass, however, I became intrigued by the genre. Not enough to keep my eyes uncovered when the scary parts arrived in *The Sixth Sense* (Shyamalan, 1999) or *The X-Files* (Fox, 1993-2002; 2016-2018). But enough to watch a few horror movies and to want more.

Over time, old favourites faded in favour of new interests and my tastes became progressively darker, until I reached a point where mainstream horror rarely "did it" for me. I still read/watch it; I still enjoy it. But, too often, it falls short of chilling me in the way that came so easily when I was young.

Eventually, I came to appreciate some of the other elements of great horror: the story, the action, the characterization. But, in the end, my desire still remains purely locked upon the need to feel fear. A horror novel can be a great book without scaring me, but it can't be a great horror novel.

And, I make things more difficult for myself. I'm at a point where very few things scare me, anymore.

Ghosts, always, because natural, human, scientific doubt in the possibility of their existence is always overthrown by the sense that there's one in the room with you when you turn out the lights. And horrible people, because they're undeniably real. Horrible people doing awful and vicious things. Maybe, on occasion, an unseen creature or a psychological condition may bring the goosebumps to the surface of my skin, but it's difficult. The rest...sorry, they just don't scare me.

Horror is an oft-spurned genre amongst analysts and critics. It's too visceral, too fake. The ability to capture that which is real, human, emotional, personal—that is what makes for great literature. I disagree. Not that those elements can't form great literature—they often do—but I disagree that those are the sole permissible elements. Horror elicits a bodily reaction and often exists in realms of the unreal. This is why it finds little love.

In response to the derision the genre receives due to unreality, I protest: all fiction is unreal. Some attempts to resemble the real, to "trick" the reader into believing that it could, really, have happened. But this doesn't make it any more real than a work of horror, fantasy, mystery, melodrama, or science fiction. That some takes on the guise of reality does not make it "better" than that which does not. Any type of literature can make observations on life or politics or relationships or emotion. Any type of literature can emphasize plot over all other elements. The quality of the literature comes down to its effectiveness in accomplishing its own goal. No two works are precisely alike, either in content, or in intention.

When it comes to the bodily reaction element of horror, this is undeniable. The fact is that some want art to provide a purely cerebral experience. The brain, for these individuals, is the sole body part that should be exercised when engaging with a book, film, painting, etc. But isn't that, in many ways, too obvious? Of course the brain will be exercised, by default, when engaging with art, whether this occurs through the production of mental images; the extrapolations of meaning from lines and colours; the focus to comprehend a complex storyline; the ability to appreciate the minutiae of subtle musical excellence; or any other thought that extends past the present when engaging with a work of art.

But to evoke a physical response? Not only is this an accomplishment that the aforementioned "great" works do not attempt, but it is one that they may not be capable of achieving. This is not to condemn those works that focus upon their cerebral nature. But, rather, to elevate those that don't.

How, in the world, can a person become scared, a physical reaction designed to protect our species from real and immediate danger, by reading a book or watching a movie? Theoretically, it shouldn't be possible. We know, consciously, that everything we're engaging with is decidedly unreal.

Yet, we jump. We cover our eyes. We shake, feel anxious. We have difficulty falling asleep as our minds replay the images we willingly subjected ourselves to.

To me, the mark of a great book is that it affects you, whether it affects you cerebrally, emotionally, or physically. Maybe, some would argue, the cerebral works are greater because this is a more difficult area to impact in the average person.

To that argument, I must return to my earlier statement: very few things scare me, anymore.

I don't know if *Spruce Road* scared you. I hope that it did. I gave myself a few chills while writing. Maybe ghosts aren't your thing. While they may be my greatest fear in art, they're not the only horror standard that I have engaged with and, hopefully, you'll enjoy some of my other work, when it is available. Regardless of whether it scared you and passed into the echelons of the "great horror novel," I hope that, at least, it took you on a fun ride through the twists and turns of my mind.

I enjoyed writing *Spruce Road* and finished it, from conception to completion (pre-edit), in about 18 days in November 2021. That, to me, as an author, is the key to enjoying the profession: books that keep dragging me back, that I don't want to stop writing for the night. This was one such book. It certainly won't be the deepest or most original horror novel that I will ever write, but it will always have been one of the most fun.

And that's the other great thing about horror. It's fun. That's the goal. And, so long as I call myself a horror writer, that is the sensation that I wish to bring to you.

About the Author
Scott R.S. Raphael

Scott R.S. Raphael is a Canadian author and poet based out of Toronto. He has a B.A. in English and Cinema Studies from the University of Toronto. Raphael has been writing fiction and making art since he was seven years old. He entered the public eye in 2019 when he began posting selections of his poetry on Instagram. Principally an author of fiction, with particular focus upon the horror and fantasy genres, Raphael has written a diverse collection of novels and short stories. *Spruce Road* is his first horror novel.

Connect with Scott at:
https://scottrsraphael.com/
X / TikTok: @scottrsraphael
Instagram: @srsraphael

Other Books by This Author

The Hill at the Top of the Mountain

Harper Gale is a bestselling author, haunted by the ghost of her recently-deceased husband, and terrorized at work by her disrespectful superior.

Tristan Ames is a rock star, haunted by a dark secret from his past, and terrorized by his bandmates as he struggles to write music again.

Their connection is immediate, but will their personal demons, emotional instability, and fear of moving forward keep them apart?

Being on the Isthmus of Rage and Despair

"...being on the isthmus of rage and despair/all I can do is stand, and sit, and stare."

In his debut poetry collection, Scott R.S. Raphael explores the depths of the human mind through a narrator battling the throes of unrequited love, fear, death, fantasy, mental deterioration, and, of course, rage and despair.

An exploration of the human condition and the depths to which one can sink within the darkest

corners of the mind, Being on the Isthmus of Rage
and Despair reaches into what it means to live and
seeks the answers sought by many but captured by
few.

"I miss you/ And I reply,/I do too/But I'm not
sure if I'm referring to her/or to myself,/for both are
equally gone"

EXCERPT FROM: A LITTLE SLICE

The upcoming horror novel from Scott R.S. Raphael!

Emily Dresden was a normal high schooler. Popular, fun, a good student, a kind-hearted person who was looking forward to the future. So, no one can quite figure out why she tried to kill herself last September. Including Emily.

Now back at school after a long recovery, she's cut herself off from her old friends, including her best friend, Daniel, who's determined to help Emily get back to normal. But Emily doesn't think that she can ever be normal again. Not because she doesn't want to be, but because she's convinced that there's something evil inside her, warping her mind and endangering those closest to her. And clawing to get out...

WARNING: A Little Slice contains themes of death, suicide, self-harm, and mental illness, and is recommended for adult readers.

Prologue

FROM THE WATERFALL of light in the distant hall, the monster came in grey. In many ways, he looked like a man. Head held high and confident, rounded yet angular. Shoulders bony but sculpted; arms long and gangly, but swift. Much swifter than his pace, which was slow and plodding, careful and calculated, cold.

It took a few moments for Elias to realize where he was or why he felt nothing in the haze of darkness around him, eyes drawn to that sterile white light from beyond his captivity. It took a few more to process that he was not going to be able to fight. The monster shut the door behind himself, carefully, making sure to turn the handle to avoid the click.

He was smart, for a monster.

Elias meant to scream but his throat wasn't working. Dry. How long had he been asleep? He might never know.

He might have been dead, already.

In the bed to his left, he heard a boy stir from beyond the curtain. Gasp.

The monster wasted no time with this impediment. His once slow and controlled pace, directed toward Elias's bed, now quickened as he approached the foot of the one that was just beyond Elias's sight. With a violent thwack, the figure sent the boy falling back into a deep, dark unconsciousness that, in the morning, the doctors would attribute to a fall in the night or, perhaps, a lucid dream gone awry.

For now, however, he was out of the way, and the one voice that Elias had left to protect himself against this beast was silenced.

He tried to push himself up in the hospital bed, to back away and disappear through the wall as the monster turned its silhouetted head toward him. He wore some kind of boxy equipment about his entire figure, which glinted in the sharp crescent moonlight that just eked through the window to Elias's right, flickering as trees blew wildly in the way of the only source of light, smacked against the window with an ominous *clack, clack, clack*.

Returning to his slow pace, the monster approached Elias, as if trying not to wake him, but he soon realized that it was much too late.

Elias yelped, sound finally forcing itself from his throat. But not from fear—from pain. Sharp, shooting pain in his wrists. He looked down and, in the darkness, just managed to pick out the growing circles of blood, beginning to seep through the bandages that held his skin together as the stitches dehisced.

At the sight, his head started to lighten, his stomach loosen, but he had to shake those feelings away. He wasn't one to back down. He'd always been a fighter. Prided himself on it.

So why had he tried to kill himself?

No—that just didn't make sense. It wasn't him. It didn't even feel real. Had it happened at all?

Whatever the case, he couldn't let himself be owned by that thought now, not when some evil figure from beyond the gates of Hell had burst through his hospital room door and was now reaching his long and dangling arms toward him, flickering in the moonlight, threatening to take him away.

Hands of no use, Elias prayed that his arms still had enough function to save him. He shot forward in the bed, still half-seated upon the hard mattress, swinging wildly at the approaching figure.

A forearm caught his head and he stumbled back for a moment, regrouping. Elias willed himself to do the same, but there was only so much he could do from a hospital bed. He fell to his side, tried to right himself upon an elbow. But the figure was charging fast, now.

Elias struck out with a bare foot, pathetic beneath his hospital gown, but enough to buy a few more seconds.

His eyes caught the glint of the window, so near yet unreachable. How far was the drop? It was below the tops of the trees, which was something. But in the darkness, he had no idea just how tall those trees were.

Thinking had been a mistake.

While his brain had been occupied with escape, the monster had prepared his attack, lunging forward nimbly—surprisingly nimbly for a demon of the ancient order—and had latched onto Elias's ankle.

No—not a demon. A man. His eyes shining from behind some kind of reinforced plexiglass suit. In the moonlight, Elias caught flashes of dark, medium-length hair, angular eyebrows, sunken eyes, a hard jawbone sprouting specks of black stubble.

He couldn't have been more than twenty-five, nine or ten years older than Elias, but those eyes had seen a hundred years' worth of horrors. And they threatened to inflict the same upon their soon-to-be-victim.

Elias tried to scream out, once again, as that emotionless, lined face plunged toward him, overtaking his body and stealing whatever power he had left in his heart. A tiny whimper came out, so pathetic that he felt he deserved to be taken. But still, he tried to back kick with his heel as the man engulfed him, ensnared him.

Pain no longer seemed to affect the intruder, as Elias's elbows glanced off the suit, trying to break through it and crush the bone beneath to no avail. He only hurt himself against the hard exoskeleton and felt blood rushing to the surface upon every strike.

As he was wrapped up and lifted, Elias kicked, struggled, tried to slip away but felt himself slipping only into the darkness of unconsciousness as the pain shot through every ripping piece of his flesh and cried out for mercy. "W-what are…you doing?" he finally managed to scrape out of his throat. "Who are you?"

But now was not the time for answers and the kidnapper had no time to waste. He had already taken longer than intended to get this far.

The route in had been easy. Empty halls. False scrubs. No one had looked twice on their bleary-eyed rounds. And, if they had, they hadn't acted fast enough.

But soon, surely, one or another would alert security, if not enter this room in the midst of his assault and end the journey before it began. He could not allow for that.

So, as Elias cried out, fought for consciousness, the other man shut off his mind to anything but the present escape, as he drove the two of them straight for the window and slid a baseball bat from within an opening in his suit, just above the waistline.

Struggling teenager in one hand and bat in the other, the man smashed the window in one quick motion, barely noticing the shards of sharp glass that threatened their passage, as his suit protected him from all ills.

But Elias noticed, saw the jagged edges stalactiting down toward him, promising to scalp and shave, scar and slice.

And, just as they were about to burst into the night and fall God-knew-how-far, the man finally spoke, in a low, gruff, and cold—so *very, very cold*—voice. "Stop struggling if you don't want to get hurt."

He did. There was no other choice. Elias was weak and he had been overpowered. He shut his eyes and stopped moving, aside from the shakes that he could not repel.

He felt the cold night air on his face, cutting through his skin beneath the sheer gown. His heart just as cold. And his stomach fell away as they dropped to the ground. He opened his eyes just in time to meet the grass below, face planted firmly into the soil.

But he was alive, he could wriggle his toes. He could still run, if he could just get up.

The other man was prepared for this possibility—of course, he was, Elias felt stupid for even thinking that escape might have been an option. The assailant was already atop him, dragging him up. His strength was surprising, impressive.

Or maybe Elias was just weak and light from his self-inflicted anguish. Maybe this was the punishment he faced for having defaced his own body and invited death into his veins. Even if he knew, despite his actions, that he'd never wanted to die, that he still couldn't explain why he'd done it.

"If you're going to kill me," Elias began, weakly, lips barely moving in the winter's cold, "can you just get it over with?"

Silence—not just from the kidnapper, but from the world, as they burst into a forest behind the hospital and disappeared into darkness amongst the trees. He wondered if the man might not have heard him.

Despite the black, the man seemed to know where he was going, feet reinserting themselves into previously entrenched footsteps in the snow. The wind was a terror upon Elias's cheeks, lips, nether regions. But a strange delight upon his arms, so hot and bloody, now beginning to freeze over, numbing the pain away.

They were well out of civilization before the man answered, "You don't want to die. And I have no intention of killing you."

"Oh, no?" Elias tensed, anger starting to overtake him as his fear dissipated into acceptance of his situation. He tried to turn his neck around to face the figure, but he was too cold; his muscles wouldn't do what he told them to. "Why d'you think I was in there in the first place? Nothing you do can scare me."

If it were possible to hear a smirk, Elias heard it then, as the man slowed his gait and took a much easier pace to the left, down a winding path of trees that seemed, almost, to be a walkway. "Like I said. You don't want to die. I know it. You know it. The only thing you don't know is why you lost control of your body and did something you never wanted to." He laughed slightly and leaned his lips in close to Elias's ear, his breath trapped beneath his suit, but the uncomfortable proximity of his body weighing upon Elias as he neared. "I can tell you that. If you'll listen," he whispered.

"Let me go."

"We're past that, Elias. I came for you. *You*, specifically. I've been watching you. Waiting. I knew you were going to do it. It was just a matter of time." Elias felt cold but it wasn't from the weather anymore. When it was just an abduction—he didn't understand, but at least he was prepared for an out, some blackmail or opportunity to fight. That hope drained from him and left him feeling hollow.

"I was hoping," the man continued, still in his cold, sinister whisper, "that you'd do it somewhere more public, so I could access you from the start. But you just had to do it in your room, didn't you? You know, I saved your life. I was watching. I saw it happen and I tried to get in the window to get you out. Your parents weren't home. You would have bled out there on your bedroom floor. I watched the blood pooling around your wrists and seeping into your hair." He was taking pleasure in the description, in making Elias's stomach turn such that he would have vomited, if he'd only had the strength to feel his stomach, anymore.

"I smashed the glass, almost got in. But a neighbour saw me and yelled out. I didn't have a choice. They couldn't know my face or my purpose. I had to tell them. Tell them what I'd seen, to call for an ambulance. And while they did that, I disappeared, still faceless in the night. But I never stopped watching, Elias. Not when the ambulance came, not when they took you away, not when they locked you in that ward. But I was prepared. It's hardly the first hospital I've broken into and it probably won't be the last."

They emerged into a clearing around a small shack, rotted and collapsing, wooden exterior cracking from the vines that snaked through it, from years of disuse. It looked as though it could collapse at any moment, and Elias had no desire to see what further horrors it might have held in the light of day.

"Don't worry." The man smiled crookedly. "We won't be here long. Just the night. Then I'll take you away from here, to a much more secluded location. You won't have to worry about being found or about your family."

"I want to see them. Let me go!" Elias whimpered.

"No, you don't, Elias. You're a danger to them now. You may not realize it, but you are. If you want to protect them, you'll never see them again, do you understand me?"

"Why?"

"In due time." He dragged Elias across the threshold and tossed him unceremoniously upon the scratchy floorboards. He could have sworn he heard something moving beneath, skittering, squealing. "Now"—he stood over the fallen boy as he lit a candle, illuminating the fully angular nature of his young face—"we have a choice. You can be bound to the bed, taken against your will, and held captive until I'm done with you. And, believe me, that is *not* something that I want.

"Or, you can work with me, Elias. Become one with my research and embrace the potential that lies ahead. You can shake my hand and join me. At least,"—he espied the bleeding wrist—"you can shake my hand once I've patched you up." He smiled again, and it seemed less sinister this time, though Elias could not shake the discomfort he felt from the man's sunken eyes.

The darkness started to overwhelm him. The flicker of the candle hypnotized his gaze as a tiny trickle of smoke began to weave its way past his nose and into his lungs.

"W-what's in it for me?" And, though he couldn't believe he was seriously considering it, he also couldn't help himself. Something in the man's expression, his seriousness. For a monster who had stolen him, he seemed somehow genuine.

"Greatness, Elias. Pure and simple. I—we—this is how we save the world. And everyone will know my—our names." He leaned down closer as Elias started to feel faint from the smoke, felt the night starting to take him away as the blood recommenced its slow drip from his wrists and seeped into the floorboards below. "What do you say, Elias."

"Who are you?"

He grinned, he sensed victory upon the air as Elias became high with the aroma of the night. "My name is Dr. Ogilvie Thorpe. I am a scientist, a psychologist, a researcher, and a king. But, above all, I am here to save humanity from a darkness that even experts refuse to acknowledge. This is your chance to be a part of my journey. Elias: do you want to save the world?"

And, though he'd already drifted away into a deep and dying sleep, both knew, when he awoke, that his answer would be 'yes.'